The
Sluggers
Club

The Sluggers Club

A Sports Mystery

PAUL ROBERT WALKER

HARCOURT BRACE & COMPANY
San Diego   New York   London

To Little Leaguers everywhere
—P. R. W.

Requests for permission to make copies of any part of the
work should be mailed to: Permissions Department,
Harcourt Brace & Company, 6277 Sea Harbor Drive,
Orlando, Florida 32887-6777.

Library of Congress Cataloging-in-Publication Data
Walker, Paul Robert.
The Sluggers Club: a sports mystery/
by Paul Robert Walker.—
1st ed.
p.   cm.
Summary: When baseball equipment starts disappearing
from B.J.'s Little League team, he and his friends form the
Sluggers Club to investigate the crime.
ISBN 0-15-276163-2
[1. Baseball—Fiction.   2. Mystery and detective stories.]
I. Title.
PZ7.W15377Sl   1993
[Fic]—dc20   92-28201

Designed by Lori J. McThomas
Printed in the United States of America
B C D E F G

The
Sluggers
Club

1

It was the bottom of the sixth inning and we were down 8–5. We only play six-inning games in the Granada Little League, so you might say that time was running out. But I wasn't worried—there was still plenty of pop left in the lineup of Halbertson's Flowers. That's our team. We used to be Joe's Meat Market, but Joe went out of business.

Ed Obermeyer was on the mound for the Lions Club. He's a big, husky guy who started shaving in sixth grade, and he has one of the best fastballs around. But he isn't much for control, and we knew we could get to him. Especially since we were starting with the top of the order.

Nong Den slipped on his batting helmet, grabbed a bat, and walked up to the plate. Nong is one of the new Cambodian kids who live across the river, but he acts like he's lived here all his life. He speaks good English, hits for average, and runs like Rickey Henderson. He's probably the best lead-off batter in the league.

1

Nong cocked his bat and crouched, making his strike zone as small as possible. He's pretty short to begin with, so there wasn't much to pitch to. As he leaned in for the sign, Ed Obermeyer kind of scowled and grunted like he didn't like the sign or Nong or both. Then he went into his windup, and the Lions infield started chattering away: *Hey, battah battah! Hey, battah battah! Hey, battah battah battah! Swing!*

The chatter didn't bother Nong, and it sure didn't help Obermeyer. The poor guy threw the first pitch so high that it hit the backstop. The next one was in the dirt. Then he found the range and fired a fastball right down the middle.

Dave the ump shot his right hand into the air and bellowed, "Steee-rike!" Dave is definitely a great umpire. Not only that, he's commissioner of the league. No one argues with Dave.

As Nong was getting set for the next pitch, a voice behind the backstop yelled, "Hey Nong, you good Little League boy! You supposed to hit the ball."

Nong stepped out of the batter's box and glared through the backstop at a bunch of teenagers. Lately it seemed like they were always at our games, smoking cigarettes, hanging out . . . and giving Nong a hard time. It was kind of weird, because they were all Cambodian kids from across the river, just like Nong.

"Let's play ball, Mr. Den." Dave the ump likes to keep things moving.

Nong turned away from the teenagers and looked down at our manager, Mr. Farnsworth, who was coaching third. Mr. Farnsworth is a nice guy, but he's really nervous—always touching his hair or face or shaking his shoulders or stuff like that. So it's kind of hard to tell when he's giving you a sign and when he's just being nervous. Finally Nong got the message: "Swing away!"

The next pitch was right down the pike, and Nong chopped a high hopper to short. For most players, it would have been out number one, but Nong beat the throw by two steps. Like I said, he's a heck of a lead-off man. But it takes more than a lead-off single to score three runs.

The next batter was Emily Kravitz. Emily is a good second baseman and she handles the bat pretty well, but she isn't much of an RBI man. She squinted at Mr. Farnsworth, trying to decipher his nervous tics. He tugged his right ear, scratched his nose, blinked twice, and patted his left knee. The nose was the take sign.

All the tics must have confused Emily, because she bunted the first pitch toward the right side of the infield. It was actually a great bunt—and it looked like a sure single—but the ball had a weird spin, and all of a sudden it curved toward the first-base line, right in front of Emily. She just kept running and kicked it halfway across the infield.

"You're out!" Dave the ump stood at the plate with a perfect view of the base line.

From the on-deck circle, Medgar Washington looked over at me and shook his head. Wash and I have been best friends since we were two years old, so he didn't have to say anything. I knew exactly what he was thinking. Stupid. Dumb. Dumb. Dumb. Like I said, Emily is a pretty good player, but good players don't miss signs, and they definitely don't run into baseballs. It was a mental mistake followed by a physical mistake.

Wash doesn't make mistakes—mental or physical. In fact, he's the greatest player in the Granada Little League. After seven games, he was batting over .750, and he was so good at shortstop that we didn't even need a third baseman. Of course we *had* a third baseman, but he just kind of stood there while Wash covered the ground.

As Wash walked toward the plate, I followed him into the on-deck circle. Actually it's more like an on-deck area next to the dugout, and it's protected by a fence so we don't get beaned by foul balls. Anyway, Emily Kravitz was trotting back toward the dugout, and I could hear Wash mumble, "Dumb move, Emily. Really dumb."

Emily stopped and stuck her face right up to Wash's. Her voice was half angry and half crying. "I didn't see the ball."

"You didn't see the sign either. Open your eyes, Emily."

"C'mon, Mr. Washington," ordered Dave the ump, "let's move it along."

Wash nodded and walked toward the plate. When he got there, he took a quick look around the infield, just to see where the fielders were positioned. Then he stepped into the batter's box, took a couple of practice swings, and cocked his bat.

Wash has a very special bat. It's made of aircraft aluminum, which is lighter than regular aluminum and gives you extra bat speed. Wash's bat is 29½ inches long, weighs 22 ounces, and has a barrel diameter of 2⅛ inches. The top half is silver, and the bottom half is black with white tape wound right where Wash likes to hold it. The Granada Little League lets us use our own bats as long as they meet league specifications. So Wash always brings his special bat, and no one else uses it. It's not that he's selfish—it's just that Wash is a very serious hitter, and a serious hitter needs his own bat.

"C'mon, Obermeyer," Wash called out to the mound, "lay it on me."

Obermeyer grimaced and checked Nong on first. I don't know what the heck he was checking—we're not allowed to take leadoffs until the ball reaches the plate. Maybe he was just nervous with a speedy guy like Nong on base. Anyway, he finally went into his windup, and the infield started chattering away: *Hey, battah battah! Hey, battah battah! Hey, battah battah battah!*

Obermeyer snapped his arm forward and fired a hard, low fastball over the outside corner. It was a great pitch—almost unhittable—but Wash just reached out and drove it into the gap in right-center field. Nong was a cinch to score, but the right fielder threw it anyway, and Wash cruised into third.

"Nice pitch, Obermeyer!" Wash yelled, one foot on the bag. The funny thing is that he wasn't being sarcastic. He meant it. It was a heck of a pitch.

Obermeyer just grunted and rubbed the ball. He and Wash had been competing for three years, and it always seemed like Wash came out on top.

Now we were really cooking, and I guess you could say the table was set for me. Who am I? My name is B.J. Grady, and I bat cleanup. I don't hit like Wash, of course, but I maintain a solid average, and I definitely have some pop. In fact, I'm the leading RBI man on the team. Of course, it helps that Wash is always on base.

"C'mon, B.J.," shouted Mr. Farnsworth, clapping his hands, "bring him around."

"Yay B.J.! Knock him dead, tiger!" My mom has the loudest voice of all the parents on our team. It's kind of embarrassing, so I try to ignore her—especially when the game's on the line.

I stood outside the batter's box, reached down, scooped a little dirt, and rubbed it between my hands. Then I picked up my bat and stepped up to the plate. I've got my own bat too. It's made of regular aluminum, and it's a little bigger than Wash's—30 inches and 24 ounces. It's a solid silver color with a rubber grip. My dad gave it to me for my twelfth birthday.

I glanced down at Mr. Farnsworth for the sign, but I didn't pay much attention to his weird movements. When the cleanup man represents the tying run in a game situation, he's not taking or bunting or playing hit and run. Nope. It's swing away—all the way.

The first pitch was high and outside for ball one. Obermeyer looked a little frustrated, and I figured he'd come inside with the next one and try to back me off the plate. Sure enough, the second pitch was an inside fastball at the waist. I stepped toward third and caught it right in the meat of the bat. The ball took off like a shot right down the third-base line. Wash did a little dance to avoid the ball and trotted home easily. I dropped my bat and tore for first—at least I tore the best I could. I'm not a very fast runner.

When I hit the bag, our first-base coach waved me around and I headed for second. I tried to kick it into overdrive, but my legs felt clumsy. When I rounded second, Mr. Farnsworth stopped me cold, jumping and screaming, "Back, B.J.! Back! Back!" I couldn't miss that sign.

As I stood on second and caught my breath, I could hear the guys on the bench cheering and calling my name. The people in the stands too.

"That-a-way, B.J.!"

"Go Flowers!"

"Yay B.J.! Yay B.J.!" Mom was less embarrassing after a double.

"Hey B.J.!" shouted Wash. "Nice hit—but I would have scored twice."

I looked over at Wash and smiled. It doesn't bother me when he says things like that. Besides he was right.

Now it was 8–7, with one out and a man—me—on second. All we needed was a single. Of course, with me running it had to be a pretty long one, but Tony Caldero was just the man to do it. He's the biggest guy on the team. He doesn't hit for average like Wash or me, but he can definitely hit for distance. Tony uses a 32-inch, 26-ounce bat, just like some of the pros. Tony Caldero is the king of pop.

Obermeyer was mad now—really mad. The first pitch was hard and right down the pike. Tony took a big cut. Whooosh! I could feel the air at second base.

"Steee-rike one!" cried Dave the ump.

Tony can hit it a long way, but he can also miss it by a mile. The next pitch was high and outside, but Tony took a cut at it anyway. Whooosh!

"Steee-rike two!"

"C'mon, Tony!" called Mr. Farnsworth. "Wait for your pitch."

"Let's go, Tony!" I yelled. "Hit one you like!" It was good advice. The only problem was that Tony likes them all.

The next pitch was so high that even Tony had to let it go. He stepped out of the box and glanced over at our dugout. Wash was up against the fence, watching the action. He made a fist with his right hand and tightened the muscles of his forearm. It wasn't a signal like "take" or "bunt" or "swing away," but it was a signal just the same. It meant "get tough."

Tony nodded and stepped back into the box. Obermeyer didn't even bother to wait for the catcher's sign. He just reared back and fired his best hummer. It was a good one too, but Tony took a huge cut and completely murdered the ball. I stood on the bag and watched it sail over the center fielder's head like the space shuttle going into orbit. It cleared the fence by ten feet and cleared the scoreboard too. Finally it landed in the grass and rolled over toward one of the softball diamonds.

The bench and fans went crazy as Tony rounded first and loped toward second. He's a slow runner, just like me, but if you hit 'em like that it doesn't make any difference. I trotted ahead of him, touched third, and practically walked home. I was having too much fun to rush it.

On the mound, Ed Obermeyer threw his mitt into the dirt. He looked over at our dugout, his eyes flashing with anger. "One of these days I'm gonna get you, Washington!" he yelled.

Wash just shrugged and smiled. I don't know why Obermeyer was so angry at Wash. It was Tony who hit the home run.

I stepped on the plate and waited for Tony to finish his home-run trot. He loped down the third-base line, jumped on the plate, and shouted, "Eight straight!" That was our record. We were the only undefeated team in the Granada Little League. Not only that, we were the first-round champs!

The rest of the team bolted out of the dugout and swarmed around us. "Dairy Queen for everyone!" offered Mr. Farnsworth. There's a concession stand in the park, but this was a special win and it deserved a special celebration. Like I said, Mr. Farnsworth is a pretty nice guy. "Let's put away the equipment."

We all went back to the dugout and put the balls, bats, batting helmets, and catcher's gear into the two big duffel bags that carry the team equipment. I picked up my own bat and glove and put them together on the bench. The Lions Club was doing the same in the visitors dugout. Out on the diamond, Dave the ump pulled up the bases and put them into a duffel bag along with his chest protector and face mask.

"All set?" asked Mr. Farnsworth. "I can take half of you in the station wagon, Mr. Crawford will take four, and Mrs. Grady will take the rest." Mr. Crawford is our coach. Mrs. Grady is my mom. She always helps out after the games.

"C'mon, Tony," I said, "you can come with Wash and me in my mom's car."

"Sure," said Tony. "Where's Wash?"

"I don't know. He was here a minute ago." I looked around the field. It was starting to get dark and the Lions Club had already left—they weren't in a mood to celebrate. Dave the ump was gone too. Wash was over in foul territory beyond the first-base line, looking around at the ground.

"Hey Wash, let's go!" I crossed the field to see what he was up to. "We're all waiting."

"It's gone," said Wash. "I can't find it anywhere."

"What are you talking about? What's gone?"

"My bat."

"Where would your bat go?"

"I don't know. But it's definitely gone."

A thin figure appeared from behind the stands, like a ghost coming out of the darkness. We were a little startled, but then we saw that it was just Crazy Pete, a homeless guy who hangs out in the park. Pete grew up in Granada, but my dad says he got messed up in Vietnam. He's a little scary to look at—his face is hidden by a scraggly beard and he wears a long, ratty coat even in the middle of summer. But he's pretty harmless really, as long as you don't get a good whiff of him. I mean, the poor guy doesn't take too many showers.

"What's the detail, soldiers?" Pete was hanging onto the fence and looking at us through the openings in the wires.

"I'm missing my bat," said Wash, walking into the visitors dugout.

"What's it look like?" asked Pete.

"It's got a silver metal top, a black metal bottom, and white tape on the handle."

"Sounds nice . . . Never saw it."

"What's the matter, boys?" asked Mr. Farnsworth. "Evening, Pete."

Pete lifted his hand to his forehead like a salute. "Reporting for duty, captain."

When we told Mr. Farnsworth about the bat, he ordered the whole team to comb the field. Pete helped too. We spread out and covered every inch of ground—behind the backstop, under the stands, in the outfield, everywhere. But there was no sign of Wash's bat. Finally Mr. Farnsworth called us in. "C'mon, boys, it's too dark to find anything anyway. Let's get some ice cream."

"Can I come too?" asked Pete.

"Sorry," said Mr. Farnsworth. "It's just for the team."

"What about my bat?" asked Wash. It was hard to tell in the dark, but it sounded like he was crying.

Mr. Farnsworth scratched his face nervously. It almost looked like a bunt sign. "Maybe the Lions took it by mistake," he said. "I'll call the manager later tonight. Don't worry, Medgar, it'll turn up."

"It better," said Wash. "There's hits in that bat."

2

Medgar Washington is the most perfect person I've ever known. Not only is he great at baseball, he's also great at basketball, football, soccer, swimming, tennis, track, and every other sport. On top of that, he's an A student in school, and everybody likes him, including the girls—except maybe Emily Kravitz, but that's just because Wash gave her a hard time over that dumb bunt.

The truth is that Wash and I have been best friends for ten years, and in all that time I've only noticed two weaknesses. The first is his eyes. He has terrible eyes, and he can barely see without his glasses. Some guys might let that bother them, but Wash just wears prescription goggles when he plays sports and regular glasses the rest of the time. Obviously it doesn't hurt his performance.

The second weakness is more of a problem—or at least it became a problem because of the missing bat. You see, Medgar Washington is superstitious. He won't walk under ladders or step on sidewalk cracks, and when he sees a black cat he immediately looks for a white cat to balance things out. Personally, I think that kind of stuff is silly, but I go along with it because Wash is my friend. Besides, it doesn't really hurt anything.

The superstitions that drive me crazy are the ones about baseball. Wash has to stand in a certain spot and watch his mother iron his uniform before every game. Then he goes into the kitchen and eats the same pregame meal: two pieces of baked chicken, one scoop of rice, and a green salad with four tomato wedges arranged symmetrically on the top. Wash says that the tomatoes equal four hits, and the chicken and rice are for power. Personally, I think Wash is so good that he'd hit .750 even if he ate liver and onions.

"I gotta have my bat," said Wash. "I can't hit without it."

It was three days after our come-from-behind victory. Wash had called Mr. Farnsworth after the ice cream celebration and again the next night and the next night, but all he got was an answering machine. Now we were on our way to a game with Underwood Funeral Home, and Wash had nothing but a glove in his hand and his cleats hanging around his neck.

"That's ridiculous," I answered. "You could hit with anything. Besides, I'll bet Mr. Farnsworth called the other coach and found it."

"I hope so, B.J. I really hope so."

I had never seen Wash so nervous. As we reached the park and walked toward the field, he started breathing hard and little beads of sweat ran down the side of his face. The closer we got to the field, the harder he breathed and the more he sweated. Finally, he just couldn't stand it. He took off like it was the hundred-yard dash and ran all the way to Mr. Farnsworth. I trailed about thirty yards behind.

"Did you find it? Do you have it?" I could hear Wash's voice clearly as I caught up to him.

Mr. Farnsworth looked down and coughed nervously. "Oh hello, Medgar. Did I find what?"

Wash let out a long breath like he was about to explode. "My bat! Did you find my bat?"

Mr. Farnsworth scratched his cheek and cleared his throat. "Uh, no. I'm sorry, Medgar. I called Mr. Raineville last night, and he went through all the Lions Club equipment. There were no extra bats. I'm very sorry."

"Ohhhhh," Wash moaned. "I knew it. I'm history. I'll never get another hit."

"Don't be silly, Medgar. You can use one of the team bats."

"I don't want one of the team bats. I want my bat."

"Well, maybe your father can buy you another one." Wash's dad is an orthopedic surgeon, so it wasn't really a money problem.

"Don't you see?" said Wash. "A new bat wouldn't be the same. I need that particular bat. It's got all the hits."

By this time the whole team was gathered around. Everybody was kind of nervous and upset. Wash is not only our star player; he's the heart and soul of Halbertson's Flowers. Without him we would be just an ordinary team.

"You can use my bat," I offered.

"Or mine," said Tony Caldero.

14

Wash shook his head. "They're too big."

"How about mine?" asked Nong Den. "It's small." Nong didn't really have his own bat—he just used one from the equipment bag. But it was nice of him to offer anyway.

"Naw, I'll find something I can use. At least I'll try to find something." Wash shuffled over to the big green duffel bag and pulled out all the bats. He picked one up, feeling the weight and length and balance. He took a couple of practice swings, grimaced in disgust, and tossed it back into the pile. Then he picked up another one.

Emily Kravitz came up behind him, holding her own bat over her shoulder. "I'm sorry you lost your special bat," she said. "But you deserved it for being mean to me."

"Thanks a lot," said Wash sarcastically. "I really appreciate the sympathy."

"Let's go!" called Mr. Farnsworth. "Everyone out on the field."

In the Granada Little League, each team has ten minutes to practice before the game. Mr. Farnsworth hit some grounders to the infield, and Mr. Crawford hit fungoes to the outfield. I was scheduled to pitch, so I was too busy warming up in the bullpen to pay attention to Wash and his troubles. But I got a bad feeling during our pregame ritual.

Normally, we all stand in a circle, and Wash puts his right hand out and clenches his fist. Then I put my right hand on top of Wash's, and the other players put their hands on top of mine until there's just one big stack of hands. Then Wash says, "Who's gonna do it?" And we all shout, "Flowers!" It's kind of corny, but it really gets us in the mood.

15

This time we all got in a circle and waited for Wash to put his hand out, but nothing happened. It was like he wasn't even there. Finally, I nudged him and whispered, "Wash."

He looked at me like I was nuts. Then all of a sudden he remembered and put his hand into the middle, and I put my hand on top of his, and we did our ritual. But it just wasn't the same. As I walked out to the mound, I kept thinking, *This is not a good day to pitch.*

Everything started out all right. I got the first batter to bounce back to me and threw him out easily. The second man popped out to shallow center. The third guy was a dangerous hitter, and he smashed a hard bouncer into the hole between short and third. It looked like a sure hit, but Wash slanted back with that graceful style, speared it backhanded, and threw him out across the length of the diamond.

"Great play!" I said as we walked to the dugout. "Ozzie Ozzie Fernandez Ripken." That was a little joke between Wash and me. We decided that the greatest shortstop of all time would be a combination of Ozzie Smith, Ozzie Guillen, Tony Fernandez, and Cal Ripken.

Wash didn't even smile. He just kept looking straight ahead and muttered, "Yeah, at least nobody stole my glove."

Nong Den led off with a walk and Emily Kravitz followed with a single to right field. Wash stepped up to the plate looking nervous and distracted. He had a bat from the equipment bag, but it was obvious he didn't like it. Even his practice swings looked awkward. I figured he'd snap out of it when he was swinging for real, but I was wrong.

He swung at the first pitch and hit a hard grounder right to the second baseman. The fielder scooped it up and threw to the shortstop, who stepped on second and fired to first for a double play. Wash hit the bag a split second after the ball.

Nong scored from third on the play, so we were leading 1–0. I guess I should have been thankful for that, but I was too upset about Wash. In five years of Little League, including two years in the minors and three years in the majors, I had never seen him hit into a double play. Never.

"C'mon, B.J.," yelled Mr. Farnsworth, "let's get another one. Get something going."

"Yay B.J.! Go Flowers!" Good old Mom. She was embarrassing, but she never gave up.

I dug in at the plate and took my best cut, but all I could manage was a grounder to third. He threw me out with plenty of time to spare.

It was all downhill from there. Underwood Funeral Home got to me for two runs in the second and another one in the fourth. Normally that would be no big deal for a team with big-time pop, but we just couldn't get anything going. Emily Kravitz drew a walk in the fourth, but Wash kept trying new bats and nothing he did seemed to work. And without Wash, the heart of the lineup was history. Tony Caldero and I couldn't get it out of the infield.

We had one last chance in the bottom of the sixth. The score was 3–1, there were two outs, and Nong Den was on second. Wash stepped into the batter's box with his third bat of the game. Kneeling in the on-deck circle, I shouted, "Now's the time. Just one. One little hit."

Wash cocked his bat and waited for the pitch. He let the first one go by.

"Steee-rike!" bellowed Dave the ump.

"That's all right, Medgar," called Mr. Farnsworth. "Make him pitch to you. Make him pitch to you."

The next pitch was a ball outside and low. The third pitch would have been a ball, but Wash reached out and tapped it foul down the first-base line. The count was 1 and 2.

"C'mon, Wash!" yelled my mother. "Knock it out of here!"

"Let's go, Medgar. You can do it." That was Mrs. Washington. She's a little quieter than my mom.

Wash ignored the people in the stands. He ignored Mr. Farnsworth. He even ignored me. Looking out at the pitcher, he took one practice swing, cocked his bat, and waited for the pitch. It was right down the middle and belt high. Perfect. Wash swung fast and hard and strong. It was a great swing. The only problem was that he missed the ball.

"Steee-rike three! Yerrr out!"

I knelt in the on-deck circle for a long time, staring at home plate as Wash walked away and Dave the ump bent down to brush away the dirt. I couldn't believe what I had just seen. It was worse than a double play in the first inning. Much worse. It was more like an F on a test or a dead dog in the road. Maybe it was even worse than that. In the last inning, with a man on base and the game on the line, Medgar Washington struck out.

3

"We've gotta do something," I said.

"No kidding," said Tony Caldero. "But what?"

Tony and I were sitting alone in the stands, looking out at the empty field. It was about twenty minutes after the game. My mom had given me permission to stay as long as I was with Tony. He's so big, he kind of makes you feel safe. Everybody else, including Wash, had gone home. No ice cream this time.

"The way I see it, we have two choices. We can convince Wash that he doesn't need the bat, or we can get the bat back."

"Yeah," said Tony, "or we can lose the rest of our games."

"Right. So what do you think?"

"I don't know, B.J. You know Wash better than I do. It seems crazy that he can't hit without his bat."

"It *is* crazy," I agreed. "But that's Wash. Sooner or later,

I guarantee he'll start hitting again—with or without the bat. But it might take all season."

"We better find the bat."

Suddenly a voice emerged from underneath the stands. "Tha's wha' I always say. Find the bat. You gotta find the bat."

Tony and I were so surprised that we practically jumped off the bench. We grabbed our own bats and held them like clubs, ready to protect ourselves.

"Who is it?" asked Tony. "Who's there?"

A hairy face appeared at the end of the stands, just above one of the benches. "Reporting for duty, captain."

We each let out a long breath. It was just Crazy Pete.

"What are you doing under there?" asked Tony, a little anger in his voice. "You shouldn't surprise people like that."

"I regret any inconvenience I may have caused," said Pete. "But you're sitting on my hotel room."

Even from across the stands, we could smell that he had been drinking.

"C'mon," said Tony, "let's get out of here."

"Yeah." We picked up our equipment and walked down the stands, doing our best to avoid Pete.

"Good night, soldiers," said Pete. "Sleep tight."

We walked across the field and out through the center-field gate. It's never locked during the season, so we use it as a shortcut. As we headed across the park, we noticed a group of bigger kids standing over by an old tree. They were kind of in a semicircle, with one guy in the middle facing the tree. His arm was cocked back like he was about to throw something. I started walking over to see what they were doing, but Tony grabbed my wrist.

"Don't let them see you," he whispered.

"Why not?" I whispered back.

"C'mon, let's walk around this way." He pulled me in the other direction.

"What's the big secret?" I asked. "Who are they?"

"The Black Scorpions."

"The Black Scorpions? What does that mean?"

"They're a gang, B.J. From across the river."

"What kind of gang? What do they do?"

Tony kept looking straight ahead. "I don't know what they do," he muttered. "And I don't want to know."

We walked in silence. I'd never heard of the Black Scorpions, but I figured if Tony Caldero was afraid of them, I was afraid of them too.

"So what are we gonna do about the bat?" I asked finally.

"Find it," said Tony.

"Yeah, but how?"

"Beats me."

"Let's go talk to Wash," I suggested. "After all, it's his bat."

I checked in with my mom, and Tony called his mom. Then we went over to Wash's house. It's the nicest house on the block, and the best thing about it is the big rec room in the basement. There's a pool table that turns into a Ping-Pong table and an old pinball machine that Dr. Washington bought at some sort of auction. There's even a little refrigerator stocked with sodas.

Wash was lying on the couch watching a baseball game

on ESPN. When Tony and I walked in, he looked up at us and smiled. Then he remembered that he was miserable and groaned, "I'll never get another hit."

"Right," I said, trying to humor him. "Your average will slowly dwindle from seven fifty to zero."

"That's impossible," said Wash. "I've already got twenty-one hits on the season. You can't have a zero average with twenty-one hits."

"I'm sure you'll find a way."

"Seriously, Wash," said Tony. "B.J. and I have been talking, and we decided to find your bat."

"It's gone," Wash moaned. "Gone forever."

I walked over to the little refrigerator and grabbed a soda. "You guys want one?"

"Sure," said Tony.

"Naw," said Wash, "it'll just make me feel worse."

I popped the top and took a long cold drink. It tasted great, and it got my brain working. Wash is my best friend, and I suppose he'll always be my best friend, but I'd had just about enough of his misery.

"Look, Wash," I said, sitting down in a big armchair across from the couch, "you know and I know that you're a great hitter with or without the bat. Last year you batted six twenty-five . . ."

"Six twenty-eight," he corrected.

". . . six twenty-eight, and you didn't even have the bat."

"That was last year. This is this year."

"Right. And the thing to do this year is find the bat."

"It's gone," he whined, staring straight ahead at the TV.

Tony took a sip of his soda. Then he picked up his own bat and looked at Wash as if he were considering the idea of smashing him over the head. "If we work together," he said finally, "maybe we can find it."

"Yeah," I added, "we have to investigate—you know, like detectives."

Wash's miserable face lit up like a streetlamp. "Detectives?" he asked. "You mean like Sherlock Holmes?"

"Yeah, or Raymond Chandler."

"Raymond Chandler's a writer," Wash pointed out. "The detective's name is Philip Marlowe."

"Whatever," said Tony. "The point is we'll work together like detectives and find your bat."

Wash picked up the remote and turned off the TV. Then he sat up on the couch and leaned forward. Suddenly he was all business.

"The first thing we need is a list of suspects. And each suspect has to have a motive. B.J., you take notes. There's some paper and a pencil over by the telephone."

I got them and sat back down. I didn't mind being the secretary. I was just happy to see Wash acting like Wash again.

"Okay," he announced, "the first suspect is Emily Kravitz."

"Emily Kravitz?" asked Tony. "Why would she take your bat?"

"Because I criticized her for running into the ball. And she told me I deserved to have the bat stolen."

"That's ridiculous, Wash."

"Just write her down, B.J. I'm not saying she did it. I'm just saying she's a suspect."

"Okay, okay. Suspect number one: Emily Kravitz. Motive?"

Wash flashed an evil smile. "Revenge." I could tell he was definitely getting into this.

"Who else?" asked Tony.

"Ed Obermeyer."

"Now that's more reasonable," I agreed. "He's been jealous of you since we were ten-year-olds. And he even threatened to get you. I'd say he's our prime suspect."

"Let's not make any rash judgments," Wash warned. "Right now all suspects are equal."

"Okay," I said, writing on my notepad. "Suspect number two: Ed Obermeyer. Motive: jealousy."

"Good," said Tony. "Now who else?"

"What about Crazy Pete?" I asked.

"Why would Pete steal my bat?"

"I don't know, but he's always hanging around our games. Remember how he just sort of appeared out of nowhere when you were looking for it? And tonight after the game, Tony and I were sitting in the stands, talking about your bat, and who should be listening but good old Pete?"

"Hmmm." Wash took off his glasses and polished them on his shirt. It was a habit he had when he was thinking. "But what would he do with it?"

"Maybe he sold it for booze. He was definitely drunk tonight."

"Or maybe somebody *paid* him to steal it," Tony added.

"It's possible," Wash agreed. "Let's put him down."

I scratched his name on the pad. "Suspect number three: Crazy Pete. Motive: greed."

"Money," corrected Tony. "The guy's homeless. He's needy, not greedy."

"Good point." I crossed out "greed" and wrote "money." "Okay, who else?"

"Mr. Farnsworth," Wash suggested.

"Mr. Farnsworth? Now you're really being ridiculous. Why would he steal your bat?"

"I'm not sure. But he didn't seem very concerned about it."

"What do you mean?" I asked. "He ordered the whole team to look for it."

"That could have been a cover-up," Wash explained. "By that time it was already gone. And then today, when I asked him about it, he acted very nervous."

"He always acts nervous."

"But this was more than regular nervous. This was suspicious. At first he pretended that he didn't know what I was talking about. Then he said he called the Lions coach. If he really called him, how come he didn't remember it right away? And how come he never returned my phone calls? We have an answering machine on both phone lines."

"I still don't see why he would steal your bat. You're our star player and he's our manager. It doesn't make sense."

Wash got up and walked over to the little refrigerator. He grabbed a soda, popped the top, and paced the room, sipping the soda and trying to come up with a motive.

"What if Mr. Farnsworth has a gambling problem?" he asked. "You know, like Pete Rose? Maybe he's betting on our games, and he figured that by stealing my bat he'd make sure we lost?"

"That is the most ridiculous thing I ever heard. Who bets on Little League games?"

Wash shrugged his shoulders and grinned. He liked the idea of Mr. Farnsworth as a suspect, and he wasn't about to give it up. "It doesn't hurt to put him down."

"Okay, okay." I wrote Mr. Farnsworth's name under Crazy Pete's. "Suspect number four: Mr. Farnsworth. Motive?"

"This time it's greed," said Tony.

"Right. Motive: greed." I wrote it on the notepad. "If we put Farnsworth down," I reasoned, "then we might as well include Dave the ump. After all, he was there too. And he was gone by the time you discovered that the bat was missing."

"Naw," said Wash. "Dave's a cool dude. He would never steal my bat. Besides, he's the commissioner."

"Maybe he's head of the gambling syndicate," I suggested.

"Now that's *really* ridiculous."

"All right, we'll forget Dave the ump." I looked down at my notepad and read off the four suspects, one by one, along with their motives. It was actually a pretty good list, even if Mr. Farnsworth was kind of on the edge. "So, is that it?" I asked. "Anyone else?"

"I can't think of anybody," said Wash.

"Neither can I. Tony?"

Tony picked up his bat again and wiggled it up and down. It looked like there was something on his mind, but he didn't want to say it. Finally, he rested the bat on the ground and whispered, "The Black Scorpions."

"Huh?" asked Wash.

"The Black Scorpions," Tony repeated, louder than before.

"They're a gang," I explained. "From across the river."

"What's their motive?" asked Wash.

"They don't need a motive," said Tony.

"Everybody needs a motive," Wash insisted. "Without a motive there's no crime."

"Yeah," I agreed. "Besides, they weren't even at the game."

"They were at the game, B.J. They're at every game."

"I never noticed them."

"You know those guys that always stand behind the backstop and give Nong a hard time?"

"Yeah?"

"They're the Black Scorpions."

"Those guys? They don't seem so scary. They're just obnoxious."

"They're obnoxious during the daytime," said Tony. "They're dangerous at night."

"I still don't see why they would steal my bat."

Tony thought for a minute, gripping his own bat tightly in his hands. "Hate," he said finally. "Their motive is hate."

"Hate?" asked Wash. "Why would they hate me? I'm a nice guy. Besides, I'm black. I'm a minority just like them."

Tony shook his head. "No you're not, Wash. You aren't like them at all. Hey, I'm part Mexican, but I'm not like them either. We were born in America, Wash. We have nice houses and parents who have good jobs and money to buy us things. Some of those guys don't even have parents, man. They don't have anything . . . except hate."

"Gee," said Wash uncomfortably, "it makes me feel kind of weird."

"Look, I'm not saying they *do* hate you, and I'm not saying they took your bat. I'm just saying it's possible."

"Okay," Wash agreed, "put them on the list, B.J."

I wrote them on my pad, right under Mr. Farnsworth. "Suspect number five: the Black Scorpions. Motive: hate. All right, that rounds up the suspect list. What do we do now?"

"We need a name," said Wash.

"Yeah," Tony agreed, "like the Granada Detective Agency."

"Right. Only I don't like 'agency.' It's too cold and impersonal. We're more like a secret organization."

"Like the Red-Headed League," I offered.

"Yeah," said Wash, "but let's be a club instead of a league."

"How about the Investigators Club?" asked Tony.

"Too obvious," said Wash. "We need a name that is more of a cover-up. So people won't know what we're really doing."

"Yeah," I agreed, "nobody has to know we're detectives. We're just three guys from the same team, hanging out together."

"Three sluggers," Tony added. "Or at least we used to be sluggers."

"That's it!" Wash exclaimed. "That's perfect!" His eyes

had that light again. I could tell he'd made up his mind.

"What's it?" I asked.

"The sluggers." Wash put his hand out, just the way he usually does for our pregame ritual. Automatically, I put my hand on top of his, and Tony put his hand on top of mine. Behind his thick glasses, Wash's eyes were blazing with light. The old Medgar Washington was definitely back.

"From this moment forward," he announced, "we are no longer three separate people. We are one group. One team. All for one and one for all. We are the Sluggers Club. Who are we?"

Tony and I looked across at each other and smiled. Then we both looked at Wash, and he was smiling too. There was no doubt about it. We knew who we were. With one voice, we shouted, "The Sluggers Club!"

4

Emily Kravitz tapped her bat three times on the outside of the plate. Then she lifted it above her head, wiggled her shoulders, and crouched down into her batting stance.

"She's shifty, B.J. Just look at those eyes," Wash whispered to me behind his glove.

"I can't see her eyes," I whispered back. "She's a lefty." We were sitting in the first-base dugout, so all I could see was Emily's back.

"Lefties are always shifty," Wash insisted. "I'm telling you, B.J., she's our number-one suspect."

Tony Caldero leaned over and held his first baseman's glove in front of his mouth. "Keep it down, you guys. We're undercover."

Wash stood up and headed for the on-deck circle, studying Emily Kravitz all the way. He was positive that she was our prime suspect. Personally, I leaned more toward Ed Obermeyer, and Tony thought we should start with

Crazy Pete. But we were "all for one and one for all." So we decided to start at the top of the list.

The first pitch was high and outside, and Emily let it go for ball one. The next one was low, and she let that go too. Emily has a pretty good eye, so there was nothing suspicious yet. But what happened next was a little surprising.

The pitcher reared back and fired a hard, high fastball over the inside corner. Normally, that kind of pitch handcuffs Emily—she just doesn't have the bat speed to handle it. But she absolutely crushed this one right between the first and second basemen. The right fielder was shaded toward center, so it rolled by him toward the fence. By the time he caught up to it, Emily had a stand-up double.

"That-a-girl, Emily!" yelled Mr. Farnsworth. "Way to get around on it!"

From the on-deck circle, Wash looked over at me and shook his head. He didn't say anything out loud—he just formed a single word with his mouth: "Suspicious."

To tell you the truth, the way we played the rest of the game was a lot more suspicious than Emily Kravitz. Wash and I stranded Emily at second, and we never had another man in scoring position. We got shut out 4–0. I guess you could say our pop was pooped.

"C'mon, kids," said Mr. Farnsworth, "let's put the equipment away."

The whole team sort of trudged around the dugout, picking up the bats, balls, helmets, and catcher's equipment. We were practically moving in slow motion—like we were all depressed. I know I was.

When the equipment was put away, Mr. Farnsworth

knelt down to close the two big duffel bags. "That's funny," he said nervously. "I thought we had six practice balls."

"We did," said Mr. Crawford. "I counted them before the game."

"Well, there's only five now. Hmm."

Mr. Crawford turned to the team. "Check your gloves. Has anyone got a ball that doesn't belong there?"

They all checked their gloves, but nobody found the practice ball. At least nobody admitted to it.

Mr. Farnsworth glanced at his watch and scratched his nose like he was giving the take sign. "It's getting late," he said, "so we'll forget about it. Maybe the other team picked it up by mistake."

"You said that about my bat," Wash pointed out. I glanced at Tony and gave him a secret Sluggers Club smile. Wash was interrogating suspect number four.

"I know, Medgar, and I'm very sorry about your bat. But we have to put all that behind us and get back on the winning track. Remember, Tuesday's game is at seven, so let's be here by six thirty." Mr. Farnsworth and Mr. Crawford picked up the equipment bags, and the players headed home.

"You've got to follow her, B.J.," Wash whispered. "She's getting away." Wash pointed at Emily Kravitz, walking alone through the outfield. She was the only girl on the team, so she wasn't really friends with any of the other players.

"Why me?" I asked. "Why don't you follow her?"

Wash looked at me like I was hopeless. "Don't be ridiculous. If she stole my bat, then she'd be suspicious as soon as she saw me. You can just hang back, and if she sees you—no big deal—you just happen to be strolling in the same direction."

"He's right, B.J.," said Tony. "I'm too big, and Wash is the victim of the crime. But you're perfect. You blend in with the scenery."

I could see they had made up their minds, so I told my mom that I was going to walk home with Wash and Tony. That was no problem, because I usually do it anyway. As soon as my mom got into the car, I handed my bat and glove to Wash.

"Don't lose her, B.J. We're counting on you."

"Good luck," said Tony.

I nodded and took a deep breath. Then I put my legs in gear.

Emily was already through the center-field gate and half-way across the park, right near the tree where Tony and I had seen the Black Scorpions. At first I was practically running, and in a couple of minutes I closed the distance to about fifty yards. Then I slowed down and tried to match her step for step. It was my first trailing job, so I was kind of making it up as I went along.

When she reached the edge of the park, Emily walked south down Falcon Street. It was the opposite direction from my house, so I had to think of a good excuse if she happened to notice me. Of course, she wasn't supposed to notice me—not if I did a good job. But just in case, I decided to tell her that I was on my way to visit a friend.

I trailed her for three blocks along Falcon, still hanging about fifty yards behind. There were a lot of people on the sidewalk, and I just tried to blend in with the crowd. Every once in a while I stopped and crouched down behind a

parked car or leaned back against a streetlight. A few people looked at me like I was acting kind of strange, but
Emily just kept walking straight ahead. Then she threw
me a curveball.

Falcon is one of the main streets in Granada, and the
cars were whizzing by pretty steadily. But Emily just
stepped off the curb, took a quick look both ways, and tore
across the street. By the time I knew what hit me, she was
walking east on Vernon Way.

I started running to catch up, and that's when I realized
I was still wearing my cleats. They were just rubber—the
Granada Little League doesn't let us wear metal cleats—
but they made it pretty tough to maneuver on the pavement. I practically got creamed by a green Volkswagen
right in the middle of Falcon Street. It's dangerous being
an investigator.

In the meantime, Emily was halfway down Vernon Way.
I kept running along the sidewalk, narrowing the gap to
about fifty yards again. Emily must have heard my cleats
on the sidewalk, because all of a sudden she stopped and
looked over her shoulder. I dove behind the nearest cover
I could find, which turned out to be a bunch of garbage
cans. They were pretty stinky, but it was the best I could
do.

Down the sidewalk, Emily was squinting and looking
back in my direction. I could see her clearly through a crack
between the cans. From the look on her face, I was sure
she heard me, but I couldn't tell if she had seen me. Her
eyes passed over the garbage cans without any change in
her expression. Then she sort of shrugged and kept on
walking.

I scrambled out from behind the garbage cans and followed her. She was definitely suspicious now, so I walked on the edge of the lawns—that way she wouldn't hear my cleats on the sidewalk. One lady gave me a nasty look through her picture window, but other than that the lawn-walking worked out great until the end of the block. That's when Emily turned the corner and disappeared behind a humongous hedge.

I tore across three lawns and tried to cut through the hedge, but all I got was a bunch of scratches up and down my arms. Finally I gave up and ran back to the sidewalk and around the hedge. By that time Emily was a hundred yards down Kirk Terrace. If she turned again I'd lose her for sure.

It was too late to be careful, so I ran at full speed with my cleats clopping on the sidewalk. I was just closing the gap when Emily turned into a walkway and bent over to pick up a newspaper. Once I'm running, I'm kind of like a freight train—I have a hard time coming to a smooth stop. And the cleats just made it worse. So before I knew what hit me I was standing face-to-face with Emily Kravitz.

"B.J.! Is something wrong?" Her face was creased, like she was really worried.

"Uh, no," I panted, trying to catch my breath. "I was just going to visit . . . uh . . . visit a friend."

"How come you're running? Are you late or something?"

"Uh, no. I mean yes. I mean not really. No. Not at all."

She looked at me like I was talking really stupid. Which I was. Then she glanced down at my feet.

"Why are you wearing your cleats?

"Uh . . . my cleats . . . hmmm . . . my cleats—darn it! My mom must have taken my Jordans by mistake." Actually my Jordans were hanging on a peg in the first-base dugout. At least I hoped they were hanging there.

Emily sort of squinted and looked at me again like I was still talking pretty stupid. Then she sniffed a couple of times like something smelled bad—probably me. "Do you want a cold drink?" she asked. "This is my house."

"Oh . . . what a nice house." I had to think fast. I had completely blown my cover, but maybe it was a break in disguise. Yes, definitely. The best way to find out about a suspect is to enter the suspect's territory. "Sure," I answered, trying to sound casual. "I'd love a cool drink."

Emily smiled and walked toward the door. "Great. I hate going into an empty house by myself." She reached into the back pocket of her baseball uniform and wiggled around with her hand. Then she pulled out a key on an open safety pin. She closed the safety pin, put the key in the lock, and opened the door. "C'mon in."

"Do you want me to take my cleats off?"

"Are they muddy?"

I turned my soles up to check. "Naw, not really."

"That's okay, then. We don't have fancy floors or anything." Emily led me through the front hallway and into the kitchen.

"Where's your mom?" I asked.

"She works weekends. She'll be home in a while."

Emily put her glove on the counter, leaned her bat against one of the cabinets, and set her cleats on the floor. Then she opened the refrigerator and looked around. "We have ice water, apple juice, one Hansen's grapefruit, and a six-pack of Diet Coke."

"I'll take the Hansen's, if that's okay."

"Sure. Boys always drink real soda. My mom and I are strictly into diet." Emily handed me the cold can.

"Thanks," I said, taking a drink. "Ummm, that's great."

"Do you want to sit down or something?"

"Uh, sure. I guess so."

We both sat down at the kitchen table. The Hansen's really did taste great after my incognito running—not to mention six innings of miserable baseball. "That was a monster double you had today." I figured that was a good conversation opener. Besides it was true.

Emily sort of blushed and smiled. "Thanks, B.J. Y'know, I had this feeling the guy was gonna come inside on me—everyone in the league tries to jam me. So I stepped toward first and really got around on it."

"You definitely crushed it. I'm sorry I left you stranded."

"I'm sorry too. What's with this big slump all of a sudden?"

I took a sip of Hansen's and thought for a minute. The conversation was definitely heading in the right direction. "Uh . . . everybody has slumps. I mean, I don't have any excuses myself. But Wash thinks it's his bat. He's convinced that he can't hit without it."

"That's ridiculous. Wash is the best player in the whole league. He could hit with any bat."

"Of course it's ridiculous. But you know Wash—once he gets an idea, he won't let it go."

Emily sipped her Diet Coke and looked out the kitchen

window. "He's so weird sometimes. He can be really nice one minute and really mean the next. Like what he said about me running into the ball. Sure it was a mistake, but I didn't do it on purpose. And I swear Farnsworth gave me the bunt sign. At least I thought he did."

"It's hard to tell sometimes."

Emily giggled and broke into a big smile. "Yeah, he's always wiggling around and scratching like he's got ants or something."

"Or fleas." I was starting to laugh too.

"Or bedbugs." Emily was really giggling now. I had to get the conversation back on track.

"Seriously, Emily. Wash knows you're a good player. He just wanted to win the game."

Emily tugged on her baseball cap. "Yeah, well I want to win too," she said. "And I wish he'd find his darn bat so he'd start hitting again. We can't win without Wash, that's for sure."

Bingo! Either Emily was innocent or she was the world's greatest actress. "I wonder who took it," I said, trying to sound casual.

Emily shrugged. "Beats me. I can't figure out why anyone would even want it. Hey B.J., you want to see my room?"

I practically choked on my Hansen's. I don't know why—her question just caught me off guard. But then I realized that this was a perfect opportunity to finish my investigation once and for all. "Uh, sure, Emily. That would be great."

Her room was really bright and sunny, with lots of posters on the walls. They were all posters of baseball players, which didn't surprise me at all. In fact, it looked a lot like my room. But her bed was covered with this frilly pink bedspread, and there were big teddy bears propped up on the pillows. It looked just like a girl's bed. I guess that shouldn't have surprised me—after all, Emily is a girl— but it sort of took me back for a minute.

"What do you think, B.J.?"

"It's nice. Really nice. Very colorful." I noticed this one framed picture on the wall in the middle of the posters. It was a baseball player in a left-handed batting stance. He was wearing a professional-looking uniform, but I couldn't place it. "Who's that?" I asked.

"Oh, that's my dad. He played triple-A ball."

"Wow! Did he ever play in the majors?"

"Nope. He broke his leg sliding."

"That's too bad. What does he do now?"

"He's a carpenter over in Creeville. My mom and dad are divorced."

"Oh . . . uh . . . I'm sorry."

Emily shrugged. "It's not your fault. He gives me lots of baseball stuff. Wanna see?"

"Sure."

She opened her closet and pulled out a plastic bin full of equipment. There were four different bats, a couple of gloves, a bunch of balls—all kinds of stuff. And just as I'd suspected, there was no sign of Wash's bat.

"This is great, Emily. He must be a neat guy."

She shrugged again. "He's okay." As she put the bin back into the closet, I noticed some of her clothes. They were girl clothes—all bright colors and soft materials— even dresses. I don't why, but it was hard for me to picture

39

Emily Kravitz wearing a dress. She goes to a different school, so I had never seen her in anything but jeans or a baseball uniform.

"Do you want to see my baseball cards? I've got a Nolan Ryan rookie card and a sixty-one Bobby Richardson."

There was a clock on Emily's wall, and I made a big deal of looking at it. I like baseball cards a lot—in fact I've got a 1960 Roberto Clemente. But I figured the investigation was over, and I was pretty worried about my Jordans. "I'd love to, Emily, but I better get going. My mom expects me home for dinner."

"What about your friend?"

"What friend? Oh yeah, my friend. Well, actually, I'm going to pick him up at his house, and then we're going to my house for dinner." I hate telling lies. The more lies you tell, the more confusing it gets. But sometimes an investigator has to cover his tracks.

"That sounds nice. Well, thanks for stopping by." Emily led me out of her room toward the front door.

"Thanks for the Hansen's, Emily. See you Tuesday."

"Yeah. See you, B.J."

Emily stood in the doorway and watched me walk down the path toward the sidewalk. She still had her baseball uniform on, of course—even her hat. But somehow she looked different to me. Maybe it was the frilly bedspread and all those girl clothes in the closet. Or maybe it was just seeing the picture of her father and knowing that her mom works weekends.

At the end of the path, I almost walked in the wrong direction up Kirk Terrace—that would have completely blown my cover—but at the last second I remembered to walk toward the house of my imaginary friend. I figured I'd double back to the park and see if my Jordans were still in the dugout, which I doubted. My best bet was that Wash or Tony had picked them up.

I was still depressed about our miserable shutout, but I felt good about the investigation. Emily Kravitz was definitely innocent. There was no doubt about it. Not only that, she was a pretty nice girl. I couldn't wait to tell the other guys about the first discovery. I figured I'd keep the second one to myself.

5

Just as I'd expected, my Jordans were gone when I got back to the park. I hustled home for dinner and spent a pretty nervous half hour gulping down my food, thinking about the investigation, and wondering about my shoes. Finally my mom let me go, and I ran over to Wash's house. He and Tony were down in the rec room drinking sodas. My Jordans were on the floor.

"Gotta watch your equipment, B.J.," Tony warned. "There's a thief on the loose."

"No one wants his big, smelly shoes," said Wash. "It's my bat they want. So what happened? Did you find anything?"

"Yeah, tell us."

I sat on the edge of the pool table and made my official report on the Emily Kravitz investigation. Mostly I stuck to the facts: tailing her down Falcon Street and Vernon Way, losing her behind the hedge at Kirk Terrace, blowing my cover, going into her house, talking about Wash's bat at the kitchen table, and examining her baseball equipment.

"Good work," said Tony, when I was finished. "I think we can write Emily off."

Wash took off his glasses and polished them on his shirt. "I don't know. Maybe it was all a cover-up."

"I'm telling you, Wash. Emily *wants* you to find your bat. She wants to start winning again."

"Hmmm."

"Besides, I saw her baseball equipment. She's got plenty of bats of her own. She doesn't need yours."

Wash fitted his glasses back over his ears and carefully adjusted the nose bridge. I've seen him do it a thousand times, but it always makes him look like a librarian or something. "Remember the motive, B.J.," he lectured. "It's in the minutes from the last meeting. Read it, please."

I looked down at my notes and read. "Suspect number one: Emily Kravitz. Motive: revenge."

"Exactly!" Wash jumped to his feet and began to pace the room. "It doesn't matter how many bats she has. If Emily stole my bat, she stole it to get back at me, not because she needed the bat."

"Good point," said Tony.

I stared down at my notes and tried to get my thinking straight. It's hard to argue with Wash. Even when he's nuts, he's extremely logical. "Okay, I admit that the bats don't make her innocent. But I conducted the investigation, and I'm telling you that Emily didn't do it." I paused to try and add a little dramatic effect. "Either you believe me or you don't."

Wash stopped pacing and looked at me like he was sort

of confused. I could tell that I'd really thrown him a curve. "Gee," he said, "of course I believe you, B.J. I mean if you're gonna put it like that."

"I believe you too," said Tony. "You did a great job."

"Yeah," Wash agreed, "excellent. I was just trying to consider all the possibilities."

"I know, but we have to keep the investigation moving. Let's forget about Emily and check out Obermeyer."

Tony nodded his head in agreement. "Yeah. If we're gonna find the bat, we've got to keep looking."

Wash looked from me to Tony and back to me. Then he broke into a grin. "All for one and one for all."

The Lions Club played 31 Flavors on Monday afternoon. The game had already started by the time we got there. Wash noticed Nong Den in the top row of the stands behind the 31 Flavors bench, so we climbed up and sat next to him. Even though we were on a secret investigation, it would have looked suspicious if we hadn't sat next to Nong.

31 Flavors had a Cambodian second baseman who was almost as good as Nong. I didn't know the guy's name, but I'd noticed him in the stands watching our games. I guess he and Nong were friends.

"Hey Nong," said Wash, "here to watch your home-boy?"

Nong smiled and shrugged. "I got nothin' better to do."

Tony and I looked out at the scoreboard in center field. It was the top of the second. "Three to nothing already," I said.

Nong shook his head in disgust. "31 Flavors stink."

Tony laughed. "At least they always get ice cream after the game."

"I can't believe they put Obermeyer at shortstop," said Wash. He was staring at the field, concentrating on the investigation.

"They've gotta put him somewhere," I pointed out. The Granada Little League has a rule that a player can only pitch six innings a week. It was less than a week since Obermeyer pitched against us. "And besides, he's got a great arm."

"Yeah, but he can't move. I mean the dude is like the *Hindenburg*."

"What's *Hindenburg*?" asked Nong.

"It was a blimp," Wash explained. "You know, like the Goodyear blimp that flies over the Super Bowl and the World Series. Only this one crashed about sixty years ago."

Nong laughed. "That's funny, man. Obermeyer the blimp."

Just then the 31 Flavors lead-off man slapped a hard grounder into the hole. Obermeyer went back to his right and stretched as far as he could, but the ball bounced off the edge of his glove. He kept lumbering to his right, picked the ball up bare-handed, and rifled it to first. It was a great throw, but the runner was safe by a step and a half.

"What can I say?" Wash asked, a big smile spreading across his face. "Exhibit A." He cupped his hands together and shouted, "Nice play, Obermeyer!"

Out at shortstop, Obermeyer recognized Wash and shouted back, "At least I can still hit, Washington."

Wash's smile disappeared. He took off his glasses and

pretended to polish them with his shirt. It was a pretty good act, but I could tell he was just faking it.

"C'mon, Danny!" shouted Nong. "Bring him around, man!"

Nong's friend stepped up to the plate and took a couple of practice swings. He had a nice swing—short and solid. It was a lot like Nong's.

"Let's go, Danny! Wait for your pitch!"

"Is his name really Danny?" I asked. I didn't mean to be rude or anything, but it didn't sound like a Cambodian name.

Nong smiled. "Naw, B.J. His name really Dang Nee. But he likes Danny, y'know?"

"Yeah, sure. Let's go, Danny! Hit one you like." I figured a friend of Nong's was a friend of mine. And besides, the Lions Club was our number-one rival.

Danny took a good cut at the first pitch and fouled it straight into the backstop. A bunch of voices started teasing him.

"Ouch! You almost hurt me, Little League boy!"

"Hey Dang Nee, you be more careful next time."

"Maybe you don't swing."

"That will be better!"

"And safer for everyone!"

It was the Black Scorpions. I hadn't noticed them before because the backstop was in the shadows. I still couldn't really see them, but their voices were plenty loud. Dave the ump turned around and pointed his finger at them.

"I want you boys to pipe down," he ordered. "If you can't watch politely, then don't watch at all." Dave is a big guy, and—like I said—he's the commissioner, so none of the Little Leaguers argue with him. But the Black Scorpions weren't Little Leaguers.

"So sorry, Mr. Umpire," said one of the voices. "We gonna be good Little League boys."

"Just like Dang Nee."

"And Nong Den."

"They very good Little League boys."

"Play ball!" Dave shouted, turning away from the backstop.

Danny stepped back into the batter's box and faced the pitcher. The Black Scorpions were quiet for the moment. I guess they'd had their fun. One thing for sure—they definitely rattled Danny. He swung at two pitches way outside the strike zone and struck out to end the inning.

"That's okay, Danny," called Nong Den, "you get 'em next time."

"What's with those guys, anyway?" I asked.

Nong Den's face turned blank, like he had no idea what I was talking about. "What guys?"

"The Black Scorpions."

"Forget it, B.J.," whispered Tony.

"Who told you they the Black Scorpions?" asked Nong.

"What difference does it make? I just wonder why they act like that."

Nong looked out at the baseball field. Danny was back at second, fielding a practice throw from the first baseman. "They think Danny too American," Nong explained quietly. "Me too. They think we forget Cambodia."

"But you live in America now," said Wash. "I mean you're just like us."

Nong smiled, but it wasn't really a happy smile. "Yeah,

Wash, I'm just like you. I gonna be an American. But I never forget Cambodia." He glanced down at his feet and mumbled, "Cambodia is very beautiful, but too much fighting. Always fighting."

"What kind of fighting?" I asked.

Nong looked me directly in the eyes. "Civil war, B.J. Just like American Civil War, only worse. Look, man, I rather not talk about it. Okay?"

"Yeah sure, Nong. I just wondered."

The rest of the game was pretty boring, especially if you were rooting for 31 Flavors. The Lions scored two more runs in the fourth and another one in the fifth. 31 Flavors scored once in the sixth, but it didn't make any difference. The truth is that the Lions had a great team, even without Obermeyer on the mound. There was only one team in the Granada Little League who could beat them. And that was us—Halbertson's Flowers—the real Halbertson's Flowers with the real pop and the real Medgar Washington.

"Here he comes," Wash whispered. "Watch every move."

Obermeyer crossed the infield from shortstop and stepped up to the fence in front of the stands. He stuck his ugly face up against the fence and smiled at us. "The four Flowers all in a row. Just like a garden." His voice was really sarcastic.

"At least we look good," said Wash.

"At least I win," Obermeyer replied.

"We beat your butt," Wash came back. He was getting angry, and some of the parents in the stands were looking at him.

Obermeyer shrugged his shoulders. "You got lucky. Big

Tony closed his eyes and took a cut. The ball just happened to be there."

"I crushed it," said Tony angrily. "And I'll crush it next time."

"We'll see. Anyway that's old history. It's the second half and it's a new season. The way I read the standings, we're two and zip, you're zip and two. You guys are just losers." Obermeyer turned his back on us and walked across the infield to the Lions dugout.

"What a jerk," Wash mumbled.

Nong Den stood up to leave. "I see you guys tomorrow. I gonna walk home with Danny."

"Yeah sure, Nong," I answered. "See you tomorrow." We watched Nong climb down the stands and join Danny on the 31 Flavors bench. He's a good guy, but I was glad to see him leave. It was time for the Sluggers Club to get down to business with Obermeyer. We weren't getting anywhere by shouting insults at each other. "We've gotta confront him," I said.

"But that'll blow our cover," said Wash.

"What difference does it make? Look Wash, there's three of us and one of him. Let's just start interrogating him right here and now."

"Yeah," Tony agreed. "Let's go for it."

Wash nodded. "Okay. He's so stupid, maybe we can catch him by surprise."

6

We climbed down the stands and walked around the backstop toward the Lions dugout. The Black Scorpions were still hanging around, but they didn't pay any attention to us. I guess they were just out for Nong and Danny.

No one is supposed to be in the dugout except the players and coaches. But it was the only game of the day, and the Lions coaches and most of the players were already gone, so we just slipped through the gate. Obermeyer was sitting by himself in the far corner of the dugout, knocking the mud off his cleats with a stick. He looked up at us and flashed that obnoxious Obermeyer smile. "Hey Flowers, where's your slant-eyed buddy?"

That really pissed me off. "Shut up, Obermeyer."

Tony stepped forward so that he was practically on top of Obermeyer's head. "You say that again, and I'm gonna rearrange your ugly face." I had never seen Tony Caldero threaten someone before. It was pretty scary.

Wash squatted next to Tony and looked directly into Obermeyer's eyes. He put on a sort of phony smile and spoke in a soft, soothing schoolteacher voice. "We don't speak like that, Edward. Now be a good boy and say you're sorry." It was actually kind of funny. I would have laughed out loud if I wasn't so mad at Obermeyer for what he said about Nong.

Obermeyer looked from Wash up to Tony and then over at me. He was pretty dumb, but he was smart enough to see he was outnumbered. He scratched the stubble on his cheek and tried to smile. "Hey guys, what's the big deal? I was just kidding around."

"Say you're sorry, Edward." Wash was still being a schoolteacher.

Obermeyer put up his hands like he was surrendering to the sheriff. "All right, all right. I'm sorry."

"Thank you, Edward." Suddenly Wash's face changed and his voice changed with it—from a sweet schoolteacher to a tough cop. "Now what did you do with my bat, jerk-face?"

Obermeyer was too slow to keep up with Wash. "Huh? What bat? What are you talking about?" His ugly face looked all twisted and confused.

Wash just kept staring right into Obermeyer's eyes. "You know what I'm talking about, Obermeyer. What did you do with it. Where's my bat?"

The confusion on Obermeyer's face disappeared. Then his eyes got all angry, and pretty soon he was back to his old obnoxious self. "You're a maniac, Washington. I don't know anything about your stupid bat. Get out of my way. You too, Caldero."

51

Wash and Tony backed off and let Obermeyer stand up. He picked up his cleats and walked along the bench as if he was looking for something. Everyone else was gone by now, and the bench was completely empty. For a couple seconds he looked sort of confused again. Then he whirled around and glared at Wash.

"All right, Washington," he barked, "where is it?"

"Where's what?" asked Wash. He looked pretty confused himself.

"My glove. What did you do with it?"

Wash shrugged. "How should I know?"

Obermeyer ran toward Wash like a charging bull. Tony and I stepped up like bodyguards. Wash is super quick and coordinated, but Obermeyer probably outweighs him by thirty pounds. I didn't want to see him knock Wash into the dugout wall.

"I want my glove," Obermeyer yelled, pulling up short in front of me and Tony. "Now!"

"Calm down," Tony ordered.

"Where did you leave it?" I asked.

"It was right on the bench."

"Where on the bench?" asked Wash. I could see that his brain was already working on a new phase of the investigation.

Obermeyer looked back along the empty metal bench. "I don't know exactly. I just threw it down. Then I took off my cleats and changed into my high tops. And then you guys came over, and the next thing I knew it was gone."

"We didn't take it, Ed. Honest." Wash's voice was calm

and quiet and friendly—like all of a sudden he was Obermeyer's best buddy.

"Well, I didn't take your dumb bat."

"I know. And I'm sorry about your glove."

"That's a sixty-five dollar Rawlings!" Obermeyer's face got all pouty.

"Let's look around," I suggested. "Maybe it's under the stands or something." I knew there wasn't much of a chance, but I really felt sorry for the jerk.

We looked under the stands next to the home-team dugout and around the third-base foul area. Then we checked behind the backstop. The Black Scorpions were gone, and there was no sign of Obermeyer's glove. Finally we looked around the first-base side, in the visitors dugout, and under the stands. All we found was a bunch of garbage and Crazy Pete, out cold and snoring away. He smelled like a broken liquor bottle.

"Should we wake him up?" I asked. "Maybe he saw something."

"Naw, let him sleep it off," said Wash. "Unless you want to wake him, Ed. It's your glove."

Obermeyer looked down at Pete and shook his head. "What's the point? He's too drunk to remember anything. Let's forget it."

Obermeyer walked back across the infield to the home-team dugout and picked up his cleats. Wash, Tony, and I started walking across the park. It was time for dinner.

"Hey Ed," Wash called, "I really am sorry about your glove. I hope you find it."

Obermeyer nodded his head and sort of smiled. "I hope

you find your bat too. I don't want any excuses after we beat your butt."

When we were about halfway across the park, Wash stopped and shook his head from side to side. "What a complete pitiful moron," he said. "I actually do feel sorry for the guy."

"Yeah," I agreed, "but I don't like what he said about Nong."

"I think we taught him a lesson," said Tony.

Wash shook his head again and started walking. "I doubt it. He's too stupid to learn any lessons. But I think we learned a lesson. Maybe two lessons."

"He didn't take your bat."

"Right, B.J. That's lesson number one. He's not smart enough to lie, especially after we caught him by surprise."

"So what's lesson number two?" asked Tony.

"Let's talk about it." Wash walked over to a playground near the edge of the park. It's for little kids—baby swings, a sandbox, yellow slides, orange tunnels, and plastic animals. It was completely empty. All the little kids were at home eating dinner, which was where we were supposed to be. But this lesson number two sounded interesting.

Wash sat down on top of a plastic turtle. He looked pretty funny, sort of like Yertle the Turtle. I tried sitting on a plastic pelican, but it was way too small, so I just sat on the edge of the sandbox. Tony plopped down beside me.

"Lesson number two," Wash began, "is that this is more complicated than we thought."

"What do you mean?" asked Tony.

Wash took off his glasses and polished them on his shirt. Those had to be the most polished glasses in Granada. Maybe in the world. "What I mean," he said, "is that we've been working under the wrong assumption. We've been thinking that someone stole my bat because it was *my* bat. At least that's what I've been thinking."

"Me too," I agreed.

"Yeah," said Tony. "We figured someone wanted to get you. Or maybe they wanted your bat because it's special."

Wash set his glasses back around his ears and adjusted the nose bridge. "It is special, but it's only special to me. It's only got hits for me."

"Whoa, Wash. You're gettin' pretty cosmic here." Wash is the smartest guy I know, and I really respect his ideas, but sometimes I think he's gonna take off for Mars or something.

Wash thumped on the back of the turtle. "It's not cosmic, B.J. It's the truth. I mean, sure my bat's a really nice bat, and it was pretty expensive, but it's only really special to me. To someone else it's just a bat. A very good bat . . . but still just a bat."

I scooped up some sand and watched it run through my fingers. Wash was definitely onto something, but I couldn't quite get it straight. Then suddenly it came to me. "Like Obermeyer's glove is just a glove."

Wash smacked the back of the turtle and smiled. "Exactly. It's a good glove, and it's an expensive glove, but it's just a glove. I mean, look, if someone stole my bat, then maybe the thief doesn't like me. And if someone stole

Obermeyer's glove, then maybe the thief doesn't like Obermeyer. But if the thief stole from both of us, it has to be for the equipment."

"Unless someone hates both of you," I pointed out. It was weird logic, but it made sense.

"Right. But that's impossible, because Obermeyer and I are completely different. No one hates both of us."

Tony had been listening quietly to our cosmic debate. When we were done, he picked up some sand and rubbed it between his hands. "What about the Black Scorpions?" he asked.

Wash looked at Tony like he had come in out of the bullpen. "What about them?"

"Maybe they hate you both."

Wash thought for a few seconds. "Naw, you heard what Nong said. They just have this thing against him and Danny. It doesn't have anything to do with us."

"They're on the list, Wash. And remember the motive."

I didn't need to look at my notes. I could recite from memory: "Suspect number five: the Black Scorpions. Motive: hate."

Wash jumped off the turtle's back and started pacing in front of us. "Look, I'm not ruling out the Black Scorpions. I'm not ruling out anybody except Obermeyer and Emily Kravitz, because they're the only ones we've investigated. I'm just saying that I don't think the thief took the bat and the glove because of any personal feelings for me and Obermeyer. I think he—or she—took them because he wanted the bat and glove."

"What about the practice ball?" I asked. "That might have been stolen too."

Wash stopped for a moment and kicked the sand around. "I don't know. Maybe it's just a red herring."

"A red what?" asked Tony.

"Herring. Mysteries always have a red herring to throw you off the real trail. I mean the practice ball was kind of old and beat up. It doesn't seem like it was worth stealing."

"On the other hand," I pointed out, "maybe the practice ball is just a ball."

Wash smiled. "Cosmic, B.J. Very cosmic. Anyway, the only way we're gonna find out is to set a trap."

"What kind of trap?" asked Tony.

Wash sat back down on the turtle and polished his glasses. The sun was almost setting, and we were all going to be late for dinner. But no one was going anywhere until Wash came up with a plan. I'm not exactly a dummy— and neither is Tony—but there's no one like Wash when it comes to plans. I knew it would be a good one. And it was.

"It's simple," he said. "Tomorrow night, after the game, we leave something very valuable out where the thief can find it. Then we hide under the stands and see who takes it."

7

On weekdays, the Granada Little League plays games at five and seven. Personally the five o'clock games are my favorite, because it's late enough for a lot of parents to come but early enough so that I'm not starving. I hate eating dinner before I play, and so do most of the other kids. Of course, Wash eats his chicken before the game no matter what time we play, but that's just superstition.

Our Tuesday game was scheduled at seven, which is a great time for a crowd but a lousy time for my stomach. I'm either hungry because I didn't eat or ready to barf because I did. Anyway, the Sluggers Club agreed to eat dinner before the game so that we could stay and carry out our plan. I didn't barf, but I felt like it—especially after we lost 7–1. Actually I don't want to talk about the game. In our whole Little League career—even in the days of Joe's Meat Market—we had never lost three in a row.

When it was over, we asked our parents if we could

watch a men's softball game on another diamond in the park. I have a nine o'clock curfew, but my mom usually lets me slide a little after the games, especially if I'm with Wash and Tony. Wash's mom does the same, and Tony's parents let him stay out until nine thirty. Anyway, it was a believable story, and it bought us some extra time. Like I said, I hate lying, but what else could we do? We had a criminal to catch.

After we took care of our parents, the three of us waited behind the first-base stands until most of the players, coaches, and fans had disappeared. Then Tony casually walked back to our dugout and dropped his big first baseman's glove right in the on-deck circle. We figured that was a perfect place because it was pretty obvious if someone—like a thief—was looking, but it wasn't so obvious that an innocent passerby would notice it.

Tony came back through the dugout gate and met us behind the stands, and all three of us walked behind the backstop to the third-base side. The Black Scorpions had left early—I guess it was no fun razzing Nong if he ignored them.

We hung out for a while behind a light pole that's down the line from the third-base stands, right near the bullpen. Finally everyone was gone and the area around the field was deserted. One by one, we walked from the pole and crawled underneath the stands. The plan had begun.

"Do you see anything?" asked Tony. "Is it still there?" Tony wasn't very happy about using his first baseman's glove for bait. But Wash and I outvoted him because we figured it was big and obvious and expensive.

Wash scrambled up to an opening between the benches,

turned his baseball cap backward, and looked through his father's high-powered binoculars. He didn't really need them to see Tony's glove, but he figured they might come in handy later, when we were trailing the criminal. "Yeah, it's still there," he said. "In fact, I can read your name on the thumb: *T. Caldero.*"

"Wow!" said Tony. "Give me those things." Wash handed him the binoculars. Tony adjusted the focus and looked through an opening above Wash's head. "If I lose that glove, my parents are gonna kill me."

"You won't lose it," said Wash.

"And if my parents kill me, I'm gonna kill you. Both of you." Tony handed the binoculars back to Wash and crouched down beside us, squeezing his bat in his hands.

"You're not gonna lose it, Tony," I assured him. "I mean that's the whole idea. We'll be watching every second. Ecchh! What is this stuff?" I looked down to see what I was kneeling in. It was pink-brown and sticky and disgusting. I couldn't tell for sure, but it looked like a combination of a melted Dove bar and about half a pack of bubble gum. I took my cleats from around my neck and tried to work some of it off my knee. Then I rubbed the cleats on the ground. Surveillance is a dirty business.

"Nasty blade!" Wash exclaimed. "Monster nasty!" He was gazing through the binoculars at something beyond the center-field fence, out in the middle of the park.

"What are you talking about?" asked Tony.

"Over by the old tree. It's the Black Scorpions."

"Let me see." I took the binoculars from Wash, turned my cap around, and looked toward the big old tree. The Black Scorpions were standing around it in a semicircle, just like they were when Tony and I first saw them. There was a guy in the middle of the semicircle, facing the tree, his arm cocked back as if he was about to throw something. But with the binoculars I could clearly see the "something" in his hand. It was a knife—but not an ordinary knife. It was more like a hunting knife, with a huge, long, evil-looking blade.

"Death," I whispered. "Megadeath." That knife really got me. The guy who was holding it got me too. He was maybe fifteen or sixteen years old, with a red bandanna around his hair and a cigarette hanging out of his mouth. I'd seen him behind the backstop, taunting Nong, but I never really paid much attention to him . . . until now. His face was actually kind of handsome, but tough-looking too—like he wouldn't think twice about using that knife. And the way he handled it was really something. He held it cocked back behind his ear and looked around the semicircle, just to make sure the rest of the gang was watching, which they definitely were. Then he snapped his arm forward and whipped that big blade right into the heart of the old tree.

"Look!" Tony pulled the binoculars out of my hands and focused on the first-base side of the field.

"What is it?" I asked.

"Shhh," Wash whispered. "Watch."

I peered through a slot in the grandstand at the on-deck circle. The light was fading, and there were a couple of fences in my way, but I could still see Tony's glove sitting all by itself on the ground. I couldn't figure out what the other guys were looking at. Then I noticed some movement under the first-base grandstand, directly across from us.

After a few seconds the movement became a shape slowly emerging from beneath the stands and rising to its feet. With the dim light and the wire fences, I couldn't recognize the shape.

"Who is it?" I asked. "Can you see him, Tony?"

"Hold on," said Tony. "Let's see if he goes for the glove."

"C'mon," whispered Wash, "take the bait like a good fish."

The shape stood still for a few seconds. Then it began to shuffle toward the dugout. After two steps I knew who it was, even without binoculars. No one shuffles like Crazy Pete.

"Give me the binoculars," whispered Wash. "I want to see his face."

Tony handed Wash the binoculars. Even though it was Tony's glove, Wash was the best at reading the expression on a suspect's face. Or a criminal's.

"He sees it!" Tony whispered excitedly. "He's moving toward it!"

"What does his face look like?" I asked. "Is he surprised?"

"Not really," said Wash, the binoculars pressed against his glasses. "He's just kind of thinking about it. Considering the crime."

Pete stood outside the dugout fence, looking down at the glove. He swayed back and forth for a few seconds and steadied himself against the fence. Then he reached up and scratched his head. He looked around. Then he walked through the dugout gate, reached down very slowly, and picked up the glove.

"He's got it!" said Tony. "Let's get him!" Tony stood up too fast and smashed his head on the bottom of the stands. "Ow!" he yelped.

"Quiet! Don't blow our cover." Wash was still watching through the binoculars.

Across the field, Pete stood in the on-deck circle holding the glove in his hand. He looked around again. Then he walked through the front gate of the dugout and shuffled across the infield.

"He's getting away, and he's got my glove!" Tony's usually a pretty laid-back guy, but he was about ready to explode.

"Calm down," Wash ordered. "We'll give him a head start. Then we'll tail him."

"What if we lose him?" asked Tony.

"We won't lose him."

Wash sounded confident, but to tell you the truth it was hard to see Pete in the fading light. All I could make out was a thin shape disappearing through the center-field gate. I figured Wash could see him better with the binoculars. At least I hoped he could see him.

"All right," said Wash. "Let's go."

We crawled out from under the stands and walked quickly after Pete. The Black Scorpions were still hanging out by the old tree, but Pete circled around them and so did we. The last thing we needed was to meet up with the Scorpions and that big knife.

Once we were walking, I felt a little more confident. Pete was pretty slow, so we had no problem closing the distance until we could see him clearly, even in the poor light.

When he got to the edge of the park, Pete turned north

on Falcon Street. It was the way we always walked home, so we knew all the streets and buildings. We even knew most of the trees and bushes, just in case we had to duck for cover. So far the whole operation was ten times easier than tailing Emily Kravitz. But my heart was beating hard, and the other guys were excited too. Emily was just a suspect. Pete was a real criminal.

"Let's just grab him," said Tony. "We'll make him talk." With his big bat over his shoulder, Tony looked like a caveman detective.

Wash put his finger to his lips and stopped behind a tree, following Pete with the binoculars. Tony and I stopped too. "Get tough, Tony," he said. "This is it, man. He'll lead us right to my bat."

"And Obermeyer's glove," I added.

"All right, all right," said Tony. "But let's get moving."

We stepped from behind the tree and got back on the trail. Tony took the lead and we closed the gap to about thirty yards. That was a pretty safe distance in the dark. Besides, Pete was probably drunk. I could see his wobbly figure clearly as he passed under each streetlight. Then he would sort of disappear into the shadows until the next light.

"He's turning!" said Tony. "We'll lose him." Tony began to run, but Wash grabbed him from behind.

"I'll catch him!" Wash ran toward the corner and hid behind some bushes. He was definitely the perfect point man because he's smaller and quicker than Tony or me. Besides, he had the binoculars.

Tony and I followed behind, walking at a steady pace. When we caught up to Wash, we ducked down behind the bushes. Wash was lying on his stomach, holding the binoculars between two branches.

"Can you see him?" asked Tony.

"Yeah, no problem. He's about halfway down the street, right under a streetlight. He's mumbling to himself and looking around. He's crossing the street!"

Wash sprung to his feet and moved quickly and silently down the sidewalk. Tony and I followed behind, half walking and half running, trying to be as quiet as possible with our big clumsy feet. I couldn't see Pete anymore, but I could see Wash. Wash was following Pete—I hoped—and we were following Wash.

About halfway down the block, Wash cut across the street. After another thirty yards or so, he turned into a small side street, almost an alley really. We were near the river now, and the houses were smaller and closer together. We found Wash hiding behind a garage, peering down the side street with his binoculars.

"Where is he?" asked Tony. "Can you see him?" The streetlights on the side street seemed dimmer and farther apart.

"He's heading for the river," said Wash. "No wait— he's stopping. This is it!" Wash stepped from behind the garage and tore down the street as if he were stealing second base. It was amazing how fast he could run without making any noise. When we caught up to him, he was crouched behind an old Chevy in a driveway, watching with his binoculars over the hood. Pete was two houses farther down the street, shuffling up a path toward the front door. For a few seconds, I could see him clearly under a streetlight. Then he disappeared into the darkness.

"Can you see him?" I whispered, crouching down beside Wash. "Where is he?"

"I think he's at the door," Wash whispered back. "But I'm not sure. It's pretty dark."

"I knew it!" Tony groaned. "We're gonna lose him."

Suddenly a light went on in front of the house, and we could see Pete just as clearly as if it were the middle of the day. He was standing on the porch, holding Tony's first baseman's glove in his hand. A couple seconds later, the door opened and I heard the voice of another man. Then I heard Pete's voice. Then the other man again.

Very quietly, I set my bat and glove and cleats beside the wheel of the Chevy. I dropped to my belly and crawled under the front, trying to get a better look. The other man was behind a screen door, so I couldn't identify him. He just looked like a big, blurry shape. I couldn't really make out their words either. It was just low rumblings.

"What are they doing?" asked Tony. "Where's my glove?" He crawled next to me and tried to look around the bumper.

Wash moved over a little to get a better angle. "Pete's still got it. No wait—the door's opening and the other guy's taking the glove. I don't believe it!"

"What don't you believe?"

"It's Dave the ump!"

"What?"

"Dave the ump. He's taking the glove and—it's impossible! He's giving Pete money!"

I scrambled forward a couple of feet and scraped my back on the bottom of the Chevy. "Ow!" I yelped out loud, but I did my best to stuff it. Dave's face was still kind of fuzzy behind the screen door. All I could see for sure was his big hand and forearm, reaching out and giving Pete a couple of green bills. Pete grabbed his hand, and they shook with the money between their palms. Then Pete pulled his hand away and stuffed the money in his pocket. Finally the door closed and Pete shuffled down the path with a big grin in the middle of his scraggly beard.

"Let's grab him," said Tony. "Right now!" He still had his bat in his hands and his cleats around his neck.

"What's the point?" I asked. "He doesn't have your glove. And he doesn't have the rest of the stuff either." I crawled out from under the Chevy and sat back against the wheel. My back really hurt, and my knee was still covered with the sticky crap from under the grandstand. But I was too disgusted to worry about it.

Tony crawled around and sat beside me. We could see Crazy Pete shuffling back up the street, passing through the glowing circles of the streetlights. He was probably going straight to the nearest liquor store to spend his profits.

"He's just a pawn," said Wash, slumping back against the side of the Chevy. His body slid down the front fender until he dropped to the pavement beside us. His voice was very quiet and strange. "I can't believe it," he mumbled, nodding his head from side to side. "I saw it, but I just can't believe it."

"What are you talking about?" asked Tony angrily. "What can't you believe?"

Wash tapped his binoculars lightly on the driveway. In the glow of the streetlight, he looked like he was almost sick. "What I can't believe," he said, "is that Dave the ump is a fence."

67

8

Our next game was Saturday afternoon. It was an important game, because we were playing the Lions Club. With a 0–3 record, our second round was already pretty screwed up, but we were still the first-round champs—no one could take that away. In the Granada Little League, the first-round champs play the second-round champs in a big championship game at the end of the season. And it looked like we'd be playing the Lions. The last thing we wanted to do was give them the edge by letting them beat our butts.

The Sluggers Club tried to get psyched up for the game, but it was pretty hard. We just kept thinking about Dave the ump. To tell you the truth, we didn't know what to do. We considered going to the police, but we didn't think they would believe us. I mean we're just a bunch of kids, but Dave's commissioner of the Granada Little League. Not only that, he's a mailman.

"What a hypocrite," Wash snarled. "What a complete disgusting hypocrite." We were sitting on the bench before the game, watching Dave sweep off home plate. It was really strange to observe a known criminal going about his business as if everything was perfectly normal.

"And I thought he was a cool dude," Wash continued. "He sure took me for a ride." We were all upset about Dave, of course, but Wash took it more personally than Tony and me. Dave really knows baseball, and he knows his balls and strikes. Wash respects Dave. Or at least he used to.

"Where's my glove, scumbag?" Tony kept his voice very low. He didn't want Dave to hear him—he was just letting out his frustrations.

"Where's my bat, buttface?" Wash kept his voice low too. I hate to admit it, but Dave is such a big guy that we were afraid to say anything to him.

"So what are we gonna do?" I asked.

Tony lifted his bat like he was about to tee off on a slow fastball. "I'd like to take a full cut at his big fat head."

"Yeah, right," I answered. "You and what army?"

"I'm not afraid of him," said Tony.

"So go for it." He didn't sound very convincing to me.

"Cut it," Wash ordered. "Violence isn't gonna help anything, at least not yet. I want my bat first."

"And my glove," said Tony.

"And the rest of the equipment too," I added. Out on the mound Obermeyer was taking his warm-up pitches with an old worn glove on his left hand. His sixty-five dollar Rawlings was probably right next to Tony's glove.

"Right," Wash agreed. "Who knows how much stuff Dave has in that house?"

"*If* it's still in the house," I pointed out. "Maybe he sold it by now."

Tony smashed his bat against the concrete floor of the dugout. "Yeah, it could be gone forever."

Wash adjusted his goggles and pulled his batting gloves out of his back pocket. It was almost time for the game to begin. "You're right," he said. "We've gotta get moving. While we're moping around, he might be unloading the stuff to an equipment syndicate or something. We need a new plan."

"Quiet," I whispered. "He's staring right at us." Dave was standing behind the catcher, ready to pull on his face mask for the beginning of the game. But all of a sudden he looked right over at us as if he could hear what we were saying. His face got kind of scrunched up, like he was really thinking about something. My heart started pounding in my chest, and I squeezed the handle of my bat just in case there was trouble. Then Dave's face unscrunched and he smiled like he remembered something. He walked over to his big equipment bag, reached in, and fished around a little. When he pulled his arm out, he was holding Tony's first baseman's glove!

Dave walked over to our dugout and stood outside the fence. "Here, Mr. Caldero. A friend of mine found this lying around."

Tony's face got all bright and happy as he took the glove from Dave. Right at that moment, I don't think he cared about the investigation, which was back to square one. He was just so happy to have that glove in his hand. "Thanks, Dave. Thanks a lot."

Dave nodded seriously. "That's an expensive glove," he said. "You should take better care of your equipment. Next time you might not be so lucky." Then he walked back behind the plate, slipped his mask over his face, and shouted, "Play ball!"

Nong Den stepped in to face Obermeyer. He let the first pitch go by, which is what a good lead-off man should do.

"Steee-rike!" shouted Dave the ump. His right arm shot into the air like a rocket.

"Hey Nong, you supposed to hit the ball!"

"How you gonna hit if you don't swing?"

"Maybe you afraid to swing."

Naturally, the Black Scorpions were behind the backstop. Those guys were really something—they must have had a schedule, because they never missed Nong's first appearance at the plate. Nong didn't seem to care anymore, or at least he acted like he didn't care. He just stared out at Obermeyer and waited for the next pitch. It was a hummer right on the inside corner. Nong swung and missed by half a foot.

"Steee-rike two!"

"C'mon, Nong!" called Mr. Farnsworth. "Keep your eye on it!"

"That right, Nong. Keep one eye on ball. Keep other eye on me."

After our surveillance under the grandstand, I recognized the Scorpion with the biggest mouth—he was the guy with the knife. He was still wearing the red bandanna over his hair, and he had on baggy pants with lots of pockets. I couldn't see it, but I figured the knife was in there somewhere. Nong just kept ignoring the Black Scorpions and tried to concentrate on Obermeyer. Personally though, they were really starting to bug me.

On the next pitch, Nong hit a ground ball to the shortstop. It looked like a sure out, even with Nong's speed, but the shortstop bobbled it a couple times and Nong beat the throw by two steps. That shut the Scorpions up for the time being. I don't think they understood baseball enough to realize that it was an error.

Emily Kravitz stood outside the batter's box and looked down at Mr. Farnsworth. He did a whole bunch of weird nervous things with his hands: rubbing his chest, tweaking his nose, pulling his right ear, massaging his left eyebrow, shaking his head, et cetera, et cetera. Most of them were just nervous weirdness, but the left eyebrow was the bunt sign. I just hoped that Emily got it.

She stepped into the batter's box and tapped her bat three times on the outside of the plate. Then she wiggled her shoulders and dropped into her crouch. Obermeyer went into his windup and delivered a hard, high fastball that tailed in toward Emily's head. Emily was already squared off to bunt, but there was no way she could bunt a pitch like that. She dropped to the dirt and the ball went flying over her into the backstop.

"What a jerk," said Tony. "Throwing at a girl."

"She can handle herself," I answered. "Besides, it's the right pitch in a bunt situation."

In the on-deck circle, Wash clapped his hands. "C'mon, Emily, don't let him intimidate you."

Emily picked herself up and looked down at Mr. Farnsworth. The bunt sign was still on. She stepped back into the batter's box, did her little ritual, and got set. The infield chattered away: *Hey, battah battah! Hey, battah battah! Hey, battah battah battah!* Obermeyer delivered another high, inside fastball, but this time Emily was ready. She jumped backward and laid a pretty good bunt to the third-base side of the pitcher.

There was nothing Obermeyer could do except field the bunt and throw to first. Emily did her job. We had a runner on second with one out and Wash at the plate. As Emily trotted back to the dugout, Wash called to her, "Nice bunt, Emily. Way to go." She just kind of smiled and nodded, but I could tell that it made her feel pretty good.

Wash was feeling pretty good too. At least that's the way it looked to me, and I know him better than anybody. I think he was just so happy to find out that Dave wasn't a criminal that he temporarily forgot his bat problems. Or maybe it was having Obermeyer on the mound. Wash loves to hit Obermeyer.

Wash stepped into the batter's box and flashed a big smile at Dave the ump. Then he looked out at Obermeyer and took a couple of practice swings. "Lay it on me, Edward."

Obermeyer grunted and checked Nong Den on second. Then he looked back at the plate and fired a fastball right down the pike. Wash pounded it back up the middle, past Obermeyer and into center field. Nong was already rounding third by the time it hit the outfield grass. We were up 1–0!

I stepped into the batter's box and took two level practice

swings. I was feeling pretty good myself. It was my turn to pitch, and I already had a lead before taking the mound. On top of that, Wash was on first with one out. It was almost like the good old days. The only thing that bothered me was the Black Scorpions standing right behind me. They didn't say anything, but I could feel them. And I could feel that knife.

Obermeyer went into his windup, and Wash crouched at first base with his hands on his knees and his left foot barely touching the corner of the bag. I didn't see any steal sign from Mr. Farnsworth, but I knew Wash was ready to go. So I took the first pitch, which was a ball anyway. Sure enough, Wash put on the burners as soon as it passed the plate. The Lions catcher stood up and fired it down to second, but Wash made a perfect slide to the outside of the bag.

"Safe!" called Dave the ump, his arms sweeping the air. Some umps try to call plays like that from behind the plate, but not Dave. He was out at the pitcher's mound.

"Nice play, Edward," said Wash as he dusted himself off. "Wanna try again?"

Obermeyer just grunted and turned back toward the plate. He was really rattled now, and it was a perfect situation for me. I figured he'd just rear back and fire a hummer right down the middle of the plate—which is exactly what he did. I took a big cut and powered it into the left-center gap. Wash scored easily, and I wound up on second.

"Yay B.J.! Yay B.J.!"

"That-a-way, B.J.!" yelled Mr. Farnsworth.

I leaned over and caught my breath. Right then, I wasn't

thinking about the Black Scorpions at all. It just felt great to make solid contact again.

Now Tony stepped up to the plate, whipping his bat around. I figured Tony had to be in a great mood since he had his glove back. And I was right. He hit a long foul ball on the first pitch and took a huge cut on the second one that missed by a couple of inches. On the third pitch, he took an even bigger cut and creamed the ball over the right fielder's head. It was instant homer. I jogged home, and Tony followed me a couple seconds later. The Sluggers were back!

At least that's what I thought. I took the mound in the bottom of the first with a 4–0 lead. Now I'm not a great pitcher, but I'm not terrible either. Normally, four runs in the first would put me right in the driver's seat. But not against the Lions. And not with the Black Scorpions staring me in the face. I could see them on every pitch, right behind the backstop. Mr. Big Knife was the worst. His cruel, handsome face floated right above Dave the ump's left shoulder.

I walked the first batter on four pitches. When I walked the second batter, Wash ran in from shortstop.

"Hey man, what's the matter?"

"I don't know. I can't concentrate." I was embarrassed to tell him about the Black Scorpions.

"Settle down, B.J. We got you four runs. Just get it over the plate."

"Yeah, sure." I watched Wash trot back to shortstop and rubbed the ball between my hands. Getting it over the plate is usually a great idea. But the Lions 3-4-5 hitters are almost as good as Wash, Tony, and me. And the only way I could get it over was to take off some velocity. I don't have a whole lot of velocity to begin with, so it got pretty ugly. Their number-three man smashed a two-run double to left. Their cleanup hitter drove him in with another double. And Obermeyer cleared the bases with a monster homer to left-center. After that Mr. Farnsworth yanked me and put in Roger Pettinger, our other twelve-year-old pitcher. Roger shut them down, but the damage was done.

Ed Obermeyer is the kind of pitcher who throws bad pitches when he's rattled, but when he's in the driver's seat—watch out—he goes for the jugular. And my first-inning performance definitely put him back in the driver's seat. From the second inning, old Edward was practically unhittable and we lost 5–4. I don't know if the Lions beat our butts, but they sure beat my butt.

After the game, I sat by myself on the bench while the rest of the team put away the equipment. Mr. Farnsworth usually makes everyone help, but I guess he understood that I needed a little time alone. Even Wash and Tony gave me some space.

"Hey B.J., gimme a smile."

I looked up at Emily Kravitz. She had a big smile on her face, a really nice smile. To tell you the truth, I didn't mind talking to her.

"Hi, Emily. I'm sorry I lost the game."

Emily sat down next to me. "C'mon, B.J., you didn't lose the game. We all lost the game."

"I definitely made a major contribution."

"You sure pitched lousy."

"Thanks, Emily." One thing about Emily Kravitz is she's very honest.

"But look, B.J., what was the final score?"

"Five to four."

"The real Flowers would never lose five to four."

"What are you talking about?"

"What was the score the last time we played the Lions?"

I thought back to the game. It seemed a long time ago—before the missing bat and the Sluggers Club and the Black Scorpions. "Nine to eight."

"Exactly."

"Exactly what?" Emily Kravitz was getting almost as confusing as Wash.

"It's simple, B.J. You gave up five runs. Last time we got nine runs. If we were hitting the way we used to hit, we would have won nine to five."

I looked at Emily and smiled. "That's right! I mean, sure I pitched lousy, but the real problem isn't my pitching. It's our hitting!"

Emily smiled back. "Exactly." Suddenly her smile disappeared. "So when are you bozos gonna start hitting?"

"B.J.! Emily! Come over here." It was Mr. Farnsworth, and he sounded angry. The whole team was gathered around him near the equipment bags in the on-deck area. We walked over and joined them.

"All right, Flowers, I've had just about enough." Mr. Farnsworth's face was all red. He'd been managing our team for two years, but I'd never seen him like this. Of course, we'd never lost four games in a row either.

"I'm sorry," I said.

Mr. Farnsworth looked at me strangely. "What are you sorry about, B.J.?"

"The way I pitched. I mean sure we could have got more runs, but I still pitched lousy."

"B.J.," said Mr. Farnsworth, "I appreciate your sense of responsibility. But right now, I don't care that we lost to the Lions. In fact, I don't care if we never win another game for the rest of the season."

"How can you say that?" asked Wash.

"I can say that, Medgar, because the catcher's mask is gone. First it was your bat. Then it was the practice ball. Now it's the catcher's mask. I also understand that a glove was stolen from Edward Obermeyer on the Lions. I don't know what's going on here, but if this keeps up there won't be any Halbertson's Flowers and there won't be any Granada Little League. If anyone knows anything about this, I expect you to tell me—now."

Mr. Farnsworth looked around the team, but no one said anything. I kind of glanced over at Wash and Tony, but I didn't want to be too obvious. Anyway, we didn't really know anything. Did we?

9

"We don't know diddley." I slumped down onto Wash's couch and stared at the pool table.

"Bo knows diddley," said Wash. He was playing pinball on the other side of the room, which was kind of annoying me. I wanted to discuss the investigation.

"Maybe Bo can help us," Tony suggested. He was sitting in one of the chairs, tapping his bat against the floor.

"C'mon, guys, I'm serious. Let's review the case. One: Emily Kravitz is a nice girl who wants to win as much as we do. Two: Obermeyer is a complete moron, but he's a victim, not a criminal. Three: Crazy Pete turns out to be honest. Four: Dave the ump is not only honest, he's a great guy."

"And a great ump," Wash added. His fingers were tapping the flippers like crazy, and the machine was ringing and buzzing and flashing—he was really racking up some points.

"And a great ump," I agreed. "To tell you the truth, I'm kind of sorry we ever doubted him."

"We saw it with our own eyes," said Tony. "At least we thought we saw it."

"And five: Mr. Farnsworth is obviously innocent. He was ready to bite our heads off this afternoon."

"It could be a cover-up," said Wash. "No!" He smashed the side of the pinball machine in frustration. "Four hundred twenty-seven thousand points."

"What's your record?" asked Tony.

"Four fifty-three."

"Darn it, Wash!" I slammed my fist into the couch and jumped to my feet. I was getting pretty frustrated myself.

Wash looked at me like I had just moved into the neighborhood. "Huh?"

"We've got a criminal on the loose, and you're worrying about pinball."

"Hey, chill, B.J. I was just trying to relax. All great detectives need to relax in order to be logical. Sherlock Holmes played the violin. I play pinball."

"Okay, okay. Anyway, I don't think Farnsworth is covering up. If he is, he should get an Academy Award."

"You're probably right. Want a Coke?"

"Yeah, sure."

"Tony?"

"Yeah."

Wash went over to the little refrigerator and got three Cokes. Then he brought them over to us. That was classic Medgar Washington—just when I was really disgusted with him, he'd do something nice to make up for it.

"So what do we do?" he asked, sitting down across from Tony.

"You tell us. You're the great detective."

Wash took a sip of his Coke and stared thoughtfully into space, as though there was a message hanging above Tony's head. He took off his glasses, polished them on his shirt, and put them back on. I guess he could see the message better with clean glasses, because his face got sort of twisted and tense, almost like he was frightened. "Well," he said finally, "I don't think we have any choice."

"Yeah," Tony agreed. "It's obvious."

I held my Coke tightly in my hand. "What are you guys talking about?" Actually I knew exactly what they were talking about, but I didn't want to say it.

Wash turned away from the message above Tony's head and looked me directly in the eyes. "The Black Scorpions, B.J. They've got my bat."

Our next game was Wednesday night against Sheinbein Formalwear. Since I got pulled without getting an out against the Lions, I was eligible to pitch the whole game. But Mr. Farnsworth stuck me in left field and went with one of our eleven-year-olds. I probably should have been insulted, but to tell you the truth I was relieved. I don't think I could have gotten the ball to the plate with the Scorpions staring at me from behind the backstop. It was bad enough before, but now it was worse. We had another plan, and it was a lot more dangerous than following Crazy Pete.

Sheinbein Formalwear is one of the worst teams in the

league, and our eleven-year-old held them to three runs, which is a pretty low score for the Granada Little League. But Halbertson's Flowers were a complete embarrassing joke at the plate. Nong Den got on base twice, and Emily moved him along, but the Sluggers Club did absolutely zilch. We were so nervous thinking about what we were going to do after the game that we barely even saw the ball—at least I barely saw it. I guess Wash saw it a little, because he grounded out twice and popped up once. I struck out three times. Tony struck out twice, but that was because he only batted twice since I made the last out of the game.

"All right," said Mr. Farnsworth. "Let's clean up the equipment." His voice was kind of tired and nervous all at the same time. Actually I felt sorry for him. Mr. Farnsworth isn't like some of the managers who just want to win and don't care about the kids. But he doesn't like to lose either, and neither do the rest of us. Five in a row is a long losing streak.

"What's gonna be missing now?" Tony wondered. He picked up a bunch of bats and carried them to the equipment bag.

"Shhh," whispered Wash. "Keep your eye out for the Scorpions."

I looked around for the gang, but they weren't behind the backstop. Then I noticed a couple of them over by the water fountain, right behind the dugout. They weren't really doing anything, just hanging around. That's all they ever did. At least it seemed like that's all they did.

"That's it!" shouted Mr. Farnsworth. "This is going to stop right now. Everyone in the dugout!"

We all filed into the dugout and sat on the metal bench. Mr. Farnsworth and Mr. Crawford stood in front of us with the equipment bags at their feet. Poor Mr. Farnsworth was ready to explode.

"Flowers," he began, "I asked you to come forward if you had any information about the missing equipment. I thought maybe we could solve this problem together, as a team. But now I think it's too late for that. I think it's time to go to the police." Some of the younger kids looked really scared, like the police were going to storm into the dugout and throw them in jail.

"What's missing?" asked Tony.

"Maybe you can tell me, Tony," said Mr. Farnsworth.

"What's that supposed to mean?" Tony still had his bat in his hand. Personally, I wouldn't accuse Tony Caldero of anything.

Mr. Farnsworth scratched his face nervously and pulled at his ear. It looked like a steal sign. "It doesn't mean anything, Tony. I'm sorry. I just want the equipment returned."

"Please, Mr. Farnsworth," said Wash. "Tell us what's missing." Wash was always super-polite to adults when he wanted something. And right then he wanted information. We all did.

"Two items are missing, Medgar. A batting helmet and a bat."

"Whose bat?" asked Wash.

"It was one of the team bats."

"Which one of the team bats?"

Mr. Farnsworth looked at Wash sort of strangely. "Why is that so important, Medgar?"

Wash shrugged like it didn't really matter at all. "I just wondered."

Mr. Farnsworth turned to Mr. Crawford. "Which bat is it, Bill?"

Mr. Crawford pulled the team bats out of the equipment bag and laid them out on the floor of the dugout. There are usually eight bats, but now there were seven. "It's the twenty-six."

Nong Den jumped up from the bench. "Hey man, that's my bat!"

"I'm sorry, Nong," said Mr. Farnsworth. "You'll have to use one of the others."

"But the others too big." The twenty-six-inch bat was the smallest bat we had. Nong was the only twelve-year-old who used it. A couple of younger kids used it too.

Nong plopped down on the bench and stared at the concrete floor. "That's no fair," he mumbled.

Mr. Crawford slipped the bats back into the equipment bag and closed the top. Mr. Farnsworth looked at all of us, one by one. "Does anyone have anything to say?"

No one said a word. Wash and Tony and I didn't even look at each other. We just kept staring right down at the floor, just like Nong Den. Mr. Farnsworth is a good guy, but we sure as heck weren't going to tell him about the Black Scorpions.

"All right," he said finally. "Our Friday afternoon practice is canceled. I'd like to cancel the game too, but it wouldn't be fair to the other team. See you Saturday at twelve thirty."

Mr. Farnsworth and Mr. Crawford carried the equipment bags out of the dugout and kept on walking toward the parking lot. The rest of us filed out, one by one. No one said much of anything. We were all too depressed.

The funny thing is that Mr. Farnsworth didn't even mention the five losses or how we had completely blown the second half of the season or how the championship game would probably be a complete farce—if there even was a championship game. He didn't have to, because we knew all about it. Pretty soon, if we didn't get killed, maybe we'd know all about the Black Scorpions too.

Our plan was simple: spy on the Scorpions and follow them when they left the park. Simple, but dangerous.

We used our men's softball excuse on our parents, only this time we threw in a new twist. I told my parents I was going over to Tony's house for a few minutes after the softball game, Tony told his parents he was going over to Wash's house, and Wash told his parents he was going to my house. We figured that by the time they straightened it all out we'd have the mystery solved. Either that or we'd be dead.

Just to make it look good, we actually walked over to the men's softball diamond after our game. But as soon as the Little League field was clear, we doubled back and took our positions under the third-base stands. Wash had his father's binoculars again. We had given our baseball equipment to our parents because we wanted to travel light.

"There they are!" said Wash. His Halbertson's Flowers cap was turned backward, and he was looking through the binoculars out toward the big tree. "Gonzo—that knife is huge!"

"Great," I whispered. "That really helps my confidence."

"Hang tough," said Tony, trying to sound brave.

I looked at him strangely. "You're the one who told me they were dangerous after dark. I thought you were scared of them."

Tony turned away and stared out through the slot between the benches. "I am," he mumbled nervously. "Real scared."

"C'mon, you guys," said Wash. "This is just like being real detectives. We've gotta follow the Scorpions to their hideout. That's the only way we're gonna find my bat."

"And the other stuff too," I reminded him.

"Yeah," Wash agreed. "We'll be heroes."

"We should have asked Nong to join us," said Tony. "He knows the other side of the river."

"Naw," said Wash. "Nong's a cool dude, and they took his bat too. But we're the Sluggers Club and he's not a slugger. It's just the three of us."

"All for one . . ." I began.

". . . and one for all," Wash finished.

"Yeah," Tony said, "and all of us are gonna get killed."

I took the binoculars from Wash, turned my cap around, and focused in on Mr. Big Knife. It was almost dark, but I could still see him pretty clearly in the lights from the men's softball diamond. He was standing in the center of the semi-circle, facing the big tree, with his arm cocked back and that megadeath blade right next to his ear. He looked around at his audience and then snapped his arm down like a slot machine. Whack! The blade hit the heart of the old tree.

It was a heck of a trick; the guy definitely knew how to handle that knife. I wondered, though, what the rest of the gang got out of it. I mean, night after night they hung out and watched the knife show. Just like they were always hanging out and razzing Nong. I guess they were pretty bored or something.

"What's the duty?"

We all whirled around at the sound of a voice behind us. I smashed my elbow on the edge of a bench and practically dropped the binoculars.

"Who is it?" asked Wash. "Who's there?" It was pitch dark. The light from the men's softball diamond didn't reach to the Little League field.

"Reporting for duty, captain. Oops!" A body bumped into the framework of the grandstand. We still couldn't see him, but now we knew who it was.

"Darnit, Pete!" said Tony. "You've gotta stop sneaking up like that."

Pete ducked underneath the stands and stepped close enough for us to see him—and smell him. He still hadn't taken a shower, but at least he didn't reek of booze. "Sorry, soldiers. I was just checking into the grandstand hotel."

"Well, check in somewhere else," Tony ordered. He was still angry at being taken by surprise, but then his voice sort of changed and he added, "Please, Pete."

"Try the first-base stands," I suggested. "They're very nice."

"Good idea, captain. I could use a change of scenery." Pete was about to crawl back out, when Tony grabbed him.

"Hold it, Pete."

"You rang?"

"Well, I—uh—know you're kind of down on your luck, and I really appreciate the way you brought my glove to Dave the ump, and well anyway—here—buy yourself a cup of coffee and a hamburger or something." Tony reached into the back pocket of his uniform pants, pulled out a folded bill, and stuck it into Pete's palm. Pete slipped it into the pocket of his ratty overcoat and flashed us a big smile. The poor guy only has a few teeth left, but it was a nice smile just the same.

"Thank you, captain. That's very nice of you."

"And Pete?"

"Yes?"

"Please don't tell anyone you saw us here."

Pete nodded mysteriously. "Don't worry, soldiers. Your secret is safe with me." Then he crawled out from under the grandstand and shuffled over for a night's sleep under the first-base stands.

"Good thinking, Tony," said Wash. "We don't want him blabbing all over town." He was back in position, watching the Scorpions through the binoculars.

"How much did you give him?" I asked.

"Five dollars. It was all I had."

"He'll just buy booze," I pointed out.

"Probably," Tony agreed. "But I hope he buys food."

"They're breaking up! This is it!" Wash held the binoculars glued to his glasses and pointed through the slot in the grandstand. Tony and I squinted through the slot above him and tried to see what was going on. It was hard without the binoculars, but there was definitely some movement around the old tree.

"What's happening?" I asked.

"The leader slipped the knife into a leather case, and then he slipped the case into one of those long pockets he's got in his pants. Now he's walking toward Falcon. The rest of the guys are following. Let's go!"

10

Wash turned and scrambled out from under the stands, with Tony and me crawling behind him. Then we cut between the dugout and on-deck circle and walked across the outfield toward the center-field gate. My mouth was dry and my heart was pounding. We weren't talking about it anymore. We were doing it.

The Black Scorpions passed just outside the lights from the men's softball diamond. I could see them clearly for a few seconds, then they disappeared into the shadows. Wash was still following them with the binoculars.

"Can you see them?" I asked. I know that Wash has good vision with his glasses, but sometimes I wonder about him, especially at night.

"Yeah, barely. But let's move it a little."

We picked up our speed until we were practically running. At least Tony and I were running. Wash was jogging, so we were about even. As soon as we could see the Black

Scorpions clearly, we slowed down. We didn't want to lose them, but we didn't want to get caught either. If we could see them, they could see us.

When they reached Falcon Street, the Scorpions turned north, the same way Pete turned and the way we usually walk home. But the Scorpions weren't heading for our neighborhood—that was pretty definite. No, we figured they'd be crossing the river. Even the Scorpions had to go home sometime.

"Let's drop back a little," Wash ordered. "It's easier to follow them on the street." It was true. Pete was only one wobbly drunk. The Scorpions were a pack of guys walking straight ahead. We didn't even need the binoculars.

"Anyway, we know where they're heading," I added.

"Yeah," Tony agreed, "but where do they go from there?"

"To their hideout," said Wash. "Wherever that is."

There are only a couple of bridges from Granada to the other side of the river. One is right in the middle of downtown. It's real nice, with fancy stones and bricks and stuff. I cross that bridge all the time with my family in the car, because that's the way we go to the lake. The other side is mostly just open countryside, so there's nothing to be afraid of over there.

The second bridge is a different story. It's about two miles from the park, way past Dave's house. I've only seen it a couple of times, when I was riding my bike with Wash. It's made of stones and bricks, just like the other one, but there's lots of holes and cracks and garbage all over the place—kind of like Granada doesn't care about it.

The Cambodian people live on the other side of the

second bridge. Up to that night, none of us had ever been in their neighborhood. I don't know why exactly. It just didn't seem like there was any reason to go there. To tell you the truth, I was a little scared of the Cambodian neighborhood, even before I knew about the Black Scorpions. Now I was more than scared.

"They're turning," said Wash. "I'll run ahead."

Tony and I kept walking steadily as Wash ran down Falcon Street to the next corner. He stepped behind a lamppost and followed the Scorpions with the binoculars. It was a different street from the one where Pete turned, but it was in the same direction. They were definitely heading for the river.

"Can you see them?"

"Yeah, no problem. Wait, they're turning again."

Wash scrambled ahead while Tony and I walked steadily, all of us trying to be as quiet as possible. The Scorpions kept moving closer and closer to the river. The streets got smaller and darker and more crooked, until finally we were walking down a gravel alley. I could smell the river now, a combination of fish and garbage and nature. My dad says the river used to be clean and beautiful, but it isn't anymore.

"There it is," Wash whispered, peering down the alley with his binoculars.

"It" was the bridge. The middle was dark, and each end was lit by the pool of a streetlight. The other streetlights were broken or burned out. The Scorpions didn't need the lights, though. They just kept walking straight ahead, never turning around. They knew where they were going—this was their territory.

We practically tiptoed down the alley, trying to be quiet on the gravel. By the time we reached the bridge, the Scorpions were already on the other side.

"Well," I whispered, "this is it."

"It" was the moment of truth. My heart pounded hard, and I felt like going to the bathroom or throwing up or both. But I had to hang tough. It helped to know that the other guys were scared too. At least Tony was. I didn't know about Wash. Sometimes he gets so interested that he forgets to be scared.

"Let's go," said Wash. "They're getting away!" Wash stepped across the bridge quickly and silently, like a leopard stalking its prey. He was definitely interested.

Tony and I looked at each other and gulped. "C'mon, B.J., it's now or never."

"Yeah."

We stepped onto the bridge together and followed Wash. He was crouched behind a concrete wall on the other side, watching the Black Scorpions with his binoculars. The road from the bridge leads up a little hill into the area where the Cambodian people live. The moon was out now, and I could see the Scorpions at the crest of the hill, like a big moving shadow in the moonlight.

"I'll run ahead as soon as they cross the hill," said Wash. "You guys back me up."

"We're right behind you," I said.

"We'll be there," Tony promised.

"Okay, here I go." Wash ran up the hill, and Tony and I followed behind. When we caught up to him, he was hiding in some bushes looking down on the Cambodian neighborhood. Even in the moonlight I was surprised at how big it was. There were lots of little houses and trailers and a couple of old apartment buildings. There were even a few tents.

The Scorpions were walking down the main road, which was in pretty bad shape. The pavement was broken and there were big holes all over the place. But I guess it didn't matter much, because there weren't very many cars on this side of the river. At least I didn't see very many.

We followed the Scorpions down the main road, with Wash in the lead and Tony and me bringing up the rear. It felt strange to be on the other side of the river; everything seemed so different. There were dogs running around without leashes, and there was lots of garbage in the street—like the city never comes and picks it up. The houses were small and every single one could have used a paint job. Some of them had chicken coops right in the front yard.

Around the middle of the neighborhood, we passed a Cambodian family sitting on their porch with one bare light bulb hanging above them. There were a lot of people—maybe seven or eight—all crowded onto this one little porch. It looked like they had just finished eating dinner. It sure smelled like it, anyway. The cooking smells were different from anything I'd ever smelled before—real spicy. Anyway, there was nothing we could do except walk right by this family. Wash kept his eye on the Scorpions and walked straight ahead as if the people weren't there. But Tony and I smiled and waved, and they smiled and waved right back.

Finally, we passed through the main part of the neighborhood, and the Scorpions turned onto a gravel side road that led back up into the hills. The houses on this road were even worse—they were just shacks really. And the smell of garbage was horrible.

"I feel sorry for these people," Tony whispered.

"Yeah. The city should help them."

Wash was up ahead behind a boulder, watching the Scorpions with his binoculars. Tony and I walked toward him, trying to be as quiet as possible. Suddenly I stepped into a pothole and fell onto the gravel. "Ow!" I couldn't help myself. The sound just came out of my mouth.

"What's that?"

"Who's there?"

I lay face down in the gravel, trying not to breathe. Tony knelt motionless between me and Wash. The Scorpions were about fifty yards ahead. I couldn't see them, but I could hear them and feel them looking for me.

"You crazy, man."

"No, I hear something. For sure."

"Probably just a possum."

"Or a dog."

"Yeah, lots of dogs up here." I recognized the voice of Mr. Big Knife. "Let's go."

I could hear the shuffling and scraping of feet on gravel. The Scorpions weren't worried about making noise. They weren't afraid of anything.

"B.J., c'mon, it's okay." Tony bent down and shook my shoulder.

"Let's go. We're losing them!" Wash scrambled up the hill on the tail of the Scorpions. Tony helped me up, and we followed behind. My ankle was twisted a little, but it wasn't too bad—I've done a lot worse sliding into second base.

Tony and I couldn't see the Scorpions anymore, but we could see Wash, and we just hoped that Wash could see the gang. It was like tailing Crazy Pete, except that Pete didn't carry a monster knife.

When we caught up to Wash, he was squatting behind some bushes at a fork in the road. To the left, the gravel road continued on over a gentle slope; to the right, a dirt road led up a steep hillside. Wash was looking up the dirt road with his binoculars.

"What is it?" I asked. "What do you see?"

"This is it!" Wash whispered excitedly. "That's their hideout!" He pointed up the dirt road to a little shack perched on top of the hill. I could see it pretty clearly in the moonlight. It was really small—much smaller than my garage at home—and it was definitely in bad shape. There were planks of wood falling off the sides and other planks nailed on at weird angles. There was a window on the side to our right, away from the curve of the road, and it looked like there must be a door on the other side. A dim light glowed and flickered through the window and through the openings between the planks.

"They're all inside," said Wash. "And I'll bet my bat's in there too."

"And the rest of the stuff," said Tony.

"Wow," I whispered. "It's like a real robber's hideout."

"Let's get closer," Wash suggested. "Up by the window."

"Are you nuts?" I asked. Actually it wasn't a question. He was definitely nuts.

"C'mon, we can't see anything from here."

"Let's come back and search it during the daytime."

"You're not gonna chicken out now, B.J." The moonlight reflected off Wash's glasses like he was trying to hypnotize me.

"Yeah, B.J., we gotta do it."

"Okay, okay. I just thought we could find out more in the daytime."

"Let's go."

We walked up the edge of the dirt road in single file, bent over as close to the ground as possible. When we were about twenty yards below the shack, we cut off the road and crawled up the hillside toward the window. The ground was rough and rocky, and there were probably fourteen million lizards and snakes crawling around with us. But lizards and snakes were the least of my problems.

Wash was in the lead, and when he reached the base of the window he slid up the side of the shack so just his eyes and the top of his head were above the windowsill. Tony was next. He stood up and peered with one eye around the left side of the window frame. I did the same on the right side.

Five of the Scorpions were sitting around an old wooden table in the middle of the shack, smoking cigarettes and talking quietly. The only light was a candle in the middle of the table. A few other guys were sort of lounging around in the shadows. I couldn't see much else—no sign of any bats or other baseball equipment.

Mr. Big Knife was sitting at the table, directly facing the window. He wasn't looking at the window, though. He was looking down at the big knife in his hand and running his thumb back and forth across the blade. Even in the candlelight, his handsome face seemed cruel and cold. The guy really gave me chills.

One of the other Scorpions pointed to something beside the window. Maybe it was a spider or lizard crawling up the wall. Whatever it was, it was going to die. Mr. Big Knife lifted his knife and cocked it back beside his ear. He was just about to let it fly when all of a sudden he turned his head and stared directly at the window—directly at me!

My heart practically exploded. I whirled around and started running down the hill faster than I ever ran before. The slope was so steep that I fell flat on my face and rolled like a ball. Then I staggered to my feet and ran some more.

"B.J.!" Wash hissed behind me. "Come back!"

I didn't even turn around. When I got to the bottom of the hill, I kept running down the dirt road. Wash caught up to me where the dirt road met the gravel road. Tony was a few steps behind.

"What are you doing, B.J.?" asked Wash, jogging beside me.

"Running!" I gasped.

"Well stop it. He didn't see you." Wash reached out and grabbed my arm. I slowed down a little. Wash seemed so calm that I almost believed him.

"He looked right at me."

"I'm telling you, B.J. He didn't see you. It was too dark. He just turned away and fired the knife."

Tony caught up to us. He was breathing pretty hard "It's true, B.J. Nothing happened."

I stopped in the middle of the road and tried to catch my breath. My ankle was throbbing and my face didn't feel too great either. I reached up and wiped my hand across my cheek. Sure enough, there was blood on my fingers.

"C'mon," said Wash. "Let's go back."

I stared at him for a few seconds, trying to figure out how such a totally intelligent guy could be so completely insane. Then I shook my head and walked down the gravel road.

"What about my bat?" he asked, walking after me.

"Forget your bat."

Now Wash looked at me like *I* was nuts. "What do you mean, forget it? I need it."

I kept walking down the gravel road toward the Cambodian neighborhood. I was kind of limping now, and we were still a long way from home. It was a good thing Mr. Big Knife didn't see me, because there was no way I could have made it across the bridge with the Scorpions chasing me. It was easy for Wash to be brave; he was so fast no one could catch him.

"Look, Wash," I said, "you're my best friend and you're the best hitter on the team, and I'd do just about anything to get your bat back, but . . ."

"But what?"

"But I'm not gonna die for it."

11

Our next game was Saturday afternoon against Frangionni's Pizza. The Sluggers Club walked to the park together. After five straight losses, we should have been concentrating on the game, but we were too busy replaying the Black Scorpion disaster. Naturally, Wash figured it was all my fault.

"The plan would've worked if you didn't freak," he said. "I'd probably have my bat right now."

"I didn't freak. I acted normal. The guy was staring right at me with a humongous knife."

"Yeah," said Tony, "it's not B.J.'s fault. Besides, we don't know if they even have your bat. I didn't see anything."

"Maybe we should just forget the whole thing," I suggested.

"Forget what whole thing?" asked Wash. His voice was really innocent, like he had no idea what I was talking about. That's one of his tricks when he doesn't *want* to know what I'm talking about.

"The investigation. I mean we don't know anything, and we've run out of suspects." Actually the Scorpions were still suspects, but I didn't want to admit it.

"Yeah," Tony agreed. "Let's just concentrate on hitting for a while."

"Exactly!" I shouted. "How can we be the Sluggers Club if we don't slug?"

Wash stopped in the middle of the sidewalk and turned toward me with a sort of disgusted look on his face, as if I had just said something really stupid. "B.J., I am really surprised at you. That kind of simplistic statement is not worthy of your intelligence." He paused to take off his glasses and polish them on his uniform shirt. I could tell this was going to be a good one.

"The reason we are the Sluggers Club is because we *are* sluggers. I mean, our *essence* is to slug. That doesn't mean we always slug—we might even strike out—but that doesn't change our essence. Now you probably wonder where this essence comes from. Well, for me personally, my essence as a slugger is created by my bat, which has been stolen, which is the subject of our investigation. I don't want to sound egotistical or anything, but I figure that *your* essence as a slugger and *Tony's* essence as a slugger both depend on *my* essence, because you don't hit when I don't hit. So therefore the entire Sluggers Club depends on my bat, which we better find pretty darn soon."

At the end of his speech, Wash turned and walked toward the park. Tony and I stood on the sidewalk for a few seconds, watching him in amazement.

"He's nuts," said Tony.

"Yeah, but he's a genius. Who else could come up with an explanation like that?"

"I don't care if he's a genius or not. I'm tired of losing all the time. If he doesn't concentrate on hitting, I'm gonna concentrate on hitting him." Tony waved his bat around and started walking after Wash.

"Tony—wait!" I don't think he was really going to smash Wash over the head, but I wasn't taking any chances. "Look, Tony, I don't know about you, but I refuse to believe that my essence as a slugger depends on Wash's bat. So what I'm gonna do is forget the investigation and slug, with or without Wash." Actually Wash almost had me convinced, but I wasn't going to tell Tony.

"Okay," he said. "I'll do the same. Let's play some baseball."

When we got to the field, Roger Pettinger was warming up and it looked like his fastball was humming. I was eligible to pitch, but I was glad to have Roger on the mound, because I wanted to concentrate on slugging. It was time for the pop to get popping.

After our pregame practice, the team filed into the dugout and sat on the long bench. Mr. Farnsworth stood in front of us with the lineup card in his hand. His face was all scrunched up—like he was sad and disgusted at the same time.

"Well," he said, "does anyone have anything to say?"

It was a weird question, but we all knew what he meant. He still thought we knew more than we were telling about the missing equipment.

Mr. Farnsworth waited for what seemed like three hours, but no one said anything. Finally he just shook his head and started reading the starting lineup. "In center field, leading off, Nong Den. At second base, batting second, Emily Kravitz . . ."

Normally I don't pay much attention to the first part of the lineup, because it's always the same. After Emily comes Wash playing shortstop. Then me, pitching or playing left field. Then Tony playing first base. But something was different this time; in fact, it was so different that it actually took me a few seconds to get it straight in my brain. Mr. Farnsworth was already saying ". . . pitching and batting sixth, Roger Pettinger" when it hit me like an inside fastball: the Sluggers Club was benched.

After he finished the lineup, Mr. Farnsworth walked toward his favorite spot behind the dugout fence. Wash jumped to his feet and followed him. Tony and I followed Wash.

"Mr. Farnsworth, wait a minute!"

He stopped and turned toward Wash. "Yes, Medgar?"

"Why are you doing this?"

"Doing what?"

"Why are you benching us?"

Mr. Farnsworth blinked a couple of times and scratched his nose. "We've lost five games in a row, Medgar. I had to do something."

"But we're the best players on the team."

Mr. Farnsworth stared at Wash for a few seconds, as though he was trying to see right through him. Then he looked at me and Tony the same way. "Boys," he said, "you three are the most talented players on Halbertson's Flowers. There's no doubt about it. But along with talent comes responsibility. I expect you to be the leaders of this team, and to set a good example for the younger players."

"Everyone has batting slumps," said Wash.

"That's not the point, Medgar. The point is that you're being selfish. All you can think about is your own bat. You're letting it destroy your own season and the team's season. In the meantime, you boys are missing the real problem, which is that we have a thief in the Granada Little League."

Mr. Farnsworth turned away and looked out toward the field. The Flowers settled into their positions. Dave the ump leaned over and dusted off home plate. The Frangionni's lead-off man stepped into the batter's box, took his practice swings, and dropped into his stance. On the mound, Roger Pettinger leaned forward and looked for the sign. The game was beginning—without us.

"I don't believe it," said Wash.

"Believe it," said Tony.

"Maybe we should tell him about our investigation," I suggested. "Then he'd understand that we do care about catching the thief."

"Or thieves." Wash nodded toward the backstop, where the Black Scorpions were taking up their positions. Mr. Big Knife stood right behind Dave the ump. Even in broad daylight, the guy gave me the chills.

"I don't think they have the equipment," I said.

"We'll never know until we investigate." I could tell that Wash's brain was already clicking on a new plan.

"So what do we do now?" asked Tony.

Wash shrugged and walked back to the dugout. "We sit on the bench."

The old-time baseball players called it "riding the pine" because the benches used to be made of pine wood. I don't know what big-league benches are made of today, but in the Granada Little League the benches are made of some weird aluminum. So I guess you could call it riding the aluminum. But whatever you call it, sitting on the bench is pretty frustrating, especially since I was ready to slug. I could feel it in my muscles and my bones and my mind. I could see that white ball coming toward me in slow motion—floating in space—just waiting to get whacked.

It got more frustrating in the third inning when Roger Pettinger gave up four runs. Like I said, Roger's fastball was definitely humming, but he walked a few batters and made a couple of bad pitches and bam! Four–zip. In the meantime, the younger guys that Mr. Farnsworth put in for me, Wash, and Tony were doing absolutely zilch.

At the end of the inning, Emily Kravitz ran in from second base and stood in front of us. Her voice was angry and her face was red. "What's with you guys, anyway?"

"What do you mean?" I asked.

"Why are you sitting on the bench? We need you."

"Ask Mr. Farnsworth," said Wash.

"Are you in trouble?"

"Ask Mr. Farnsworth," Wash repeated.

Emily looked over at Mr. Farnsworth standing in the

104

third-base coaching box. Then she turned back toward us and focused right in on me. "B.J., I'm really disappointed in you. I don't know about these other guys, but I thought you were mature. I thought you were someone we could count on. And now you're letting us down." With that little bombshell, she turned and walked down to the other end of the dugout.

"Well, well, well," said Wash, "looks like you've been fraternizing with suspect number one."

"I think he's been doing more than fraternizing," said Tony.

"What are you guys talking about?" I knew exactly what they were talking about, but I wasn't going to admit it.

Wash did his best impression of Emily. "Oh, B.J., I thought you were mature. I thought you were someone I could count on."

"Give me a break. She's just mad about our losing streak."

"Sure, B.J."

In the top of the fourth, Mr. Farnsworth sent me out to left field and Tony to first base. It felt great to get into the game, but I wondered why he kept Wash on the bench. I guess he figured that Wash was the most talented player on the team, so he needed the most time to think. Mr. Farnsworth probably didn't realize that Wash is always thinking, and the more he thinks the more trouble we end up getting into.

With two out in the bottom of the sixth, we were still down four–zip and heading for our sixth loss in a row. Then Nong Den drew a walk, and Emily slapped a hard grounder through the hole between first and second. It was a perfect single in the situation, and Nong ran as soon as she made contact. We had men at first and third.

The next batter was Tony. It was kind of weird, having Tony bat after Emily, but Mr. Farnsworth was trying to shake things up. At least I think that's what he was trying to do. Anyway, Tony took a couple of monster practice swings, and the Frangionni's pitcher got a little nervous, even with a four-run lead. He laid the first pitch right across the heart of the plate, and Tony drilled it down the left-field line for a stand-up double. Nong scored easily, but Emily stopped at third.

Now it was up to me. Good old mature, dependable B.J. Grady. To slug or not to slug. Since we were three runs behind, the best I could do was tie the game. But that's what batting cleanup is all about. You do what you have to do.

As I stepped into the batter's box, I took a quick look at Mr. Big Knife, standing right in the middle of the backstop. It was a major mistake. He noticed me looking at him, and his face got really tight and tough for a second. Then it loosened up into a big smile—the coldest, deadliest smile I've ever seen. I practically had a heart attack right there in the batter's box.

"Let's go, Mr. Grady," ordered Dave the ump. "Play ball!"

I turned away from the backstop, took two level practice swings, and dropped into my stance. As the pitcher went into his windup, all I could think about was that deadly smile staring through my back . . . and the knife behind the smile. The first pitch was right down the middle, but I just watched it go by.

"Steee-rike!"

I stepped out of the box and looked down at Mr. Farnsworth at third base. He flashed me a bunch of signs, but I didn't really pay any attention. I was up there to slug, but how was I supposed to slug with Mr. Big Knife grinning through my back? I took my practice swings and waited for the pitch. It was another one right down the pike. I swung and missed by a foot.

"Steee-rike two!"

"C'mon, B.J. We need you!" Emily was jumping up and down on third base, clapping her hands together, begging me to bring her home. As I looked away from Emily, I noticed Wash leaning up against the dugout fence. He didn't say anything—he didn't have to. He just closed his fist and tightened the muscles of his forearm. It was the "get tough" sign.

I nodded and stepped back into the batter's box, took two practice swings, and waited for the pitch. Mr. Big Knife was probably grinning behind me, but I figured I could worry about him later. Right then all that mattered was that white ball floating toward me in slow motion. At least that's the way the baseball looked to me—big, fat, and slow. I stepped forward and put every ounce of my body into the swing. Kabloom! I dropped my bat and watched the ball sail high over the left fielder's head, a beautiful, towering, arcing homer.

The fans went crazy as I circled the bases. "B.J.! B.J.! Yay B.J.! That-a-way, slugger!" I definitely gave Mom something to cheer about.

When I jumped on the plate, I looked straight at Mr. Big Knife standing behind the backstop. He had that deadly smile on his face, but I just gave him a big smile of my own.

Emily and Nong were waiting for me. Nong slapped me a high-five, which for me was more like a medium-five. "That-a-way, B.J.!" Emily looked up at me—right into my eyes—and said, "Thanks, B.J. I knew you could do it." That made me feel pretty good, to tell you the truth.

I felt even better when Mr. Farnsworth told Wash to grab a bat. The only problem was that Wash didn't have the right bat to grab. He did his best, I guess—at least the best he could do without his crazy "essence." He fouled off three strikes and worked the pitcher to a full count. But then he went for an outside fastball and popped up to center field. We were heading for extra innings.

When we ran out to the field for the top of the seventh, Dave the ump sent us back to the dugout and called the managers up to the plate. The Granada Little League has a time limit if there's another game scheduled on the same field. Saturdays are the worst—with four games in a row things get pretty tight. Sure enough, Mr. Farnsworth gave us the bad news.

"Boys, the umpire has suspended the game. We'll finish it next week, starting from the top of the seventh inning. I know some of you feel frustrated, because you'd like to finish it now. But I think you should be very proud of the way you came back to tie it. I know I am."

As we started putting away the equipment, I looked out through the dugout fence. The players for the next game were already taking fielding practice. Mr. Farnsworth was right. I did feel frustrated. But I felt proud too. Proud of the way I ignored Mr. Big Knife and concentrated at the plate. Proud of the way I proved that my essence as a slugger didn't depend on Wash's bat. Proud of Tony's slugging too.

But even though I was very proud, I realized that something was missing—Medgar Washington. Maybe Tony and I could slug without Wash. Maybe we could tie the game. But we couldn't win. It was all for one and one for all. There were three sluggers in the Sluggers Club. And one of the sluggers still needed his bat.

12

"You're crazy! Out of your mind!" Tony stared at Wash like he was considering calling the men in white coats.

"We don't have any evidence," I pointed out. "We didn't see anything in the shack."

"Exactly," said Wash. "We didn't see anything because it was dark, and we never really investigated. And we never really investigated because you freaked."

We were sitting in the last row of the third-base stands. The next game had just begun, but we weren't watching the action on the field. Wash had grabbed us on the way out of the dugout and called an emergency meeting of the Sluggers Club.

"C'mon, B.J.," he said. "You got tough at the plate and hit a monster homer. Now it's time to get tough in the investigation."

Tony tapped his bat against the stands. "But we can't just march into the shack," he said. "They'll cream us."

"No they won't," said Wash. "Not if we go *right now*."

He looked over toward the backstop. The Scorpions were still standing around, watching the next game. There was no guarantee they'd stay there, but if we moved fast we could probably beat them to the shack.

"At least it's daytime," I pointed out.

"That-a-way, B.J.," said Wash. "I knew I could count on you."

"I didn't say I'd do it. I just said it's daytime."

"So what are we waiting for?"

I checked the Scorpions again. They were just hanging out behind the backstop, half watching the game and half goofing around. Mr. Big Knife was talking to a couple of girls from across the river. They were laughing and giggling. They probably thought he was a pretty cool, handsome guy.

I looked back at Wash, and he gave me his innocent waiting smile, like he was my best friend in the world— which he is—and he really needed my help—which he did. "All right," I said. "Let's do it."

"That's my man!" Wash jumped off the back of the stands and ran toward the light pole at the corner of the outfield fence. I'm no gymnast, so I climbed down one bench at a time. When I reached the bottom, I turned back toward Tony. He was still sitting at the top of the stands, tapping his bat against the bench below.

"Are you coming?" I asked.

Tony stared down at his bat for a couple of seconds. Then he stood up and climbed down the stands. "If you're going, I'm going," he said. "All for one . . ."

". . . and one for all."

We retraced our steps out through the park, down Falcon Street, and over toward the river. We walked as fast as we could, because we figured that the Scorpions might head home at any time, and every step we took gave us more time to search the shack.

When we got to the bridge, we walked right across. It wasn't scary at all, really. There's nothing like a little sunshine to make things nicer. Even the Cambodian neighborhood didn't seem so strange. The street was still full of potholes, the houses still needed paint jobs, and there were still dogs running loose and strange cooking smells in the air. But now there were little kids playing in the yards and older kids riding bikes and fathers cutting the grass and mothers working in the gardens or watching the babies. It was just like a Saturday afternoon anywhere.

We probably looked pretty weird in our baseball uniforms, carrying our bats and gloves and cleats. But nobody made a big deal about it. Most people just ignored us and went about their business. A few smiled and waved.

About halfway down the main street, we passed the same big family sitting on their porch. The father was standing out in the yard, holding a live chicken by the neck. He had a big meat cleaver in the other hand. I don't know where he was taking the chicken, but wherever it was, the situation didn't look too good for the bird. Wash just kept walking straight ahead, but Tony and I waved and the people on the porch waved back. It was like we were old friends or something.

After we passed through the main part of the neighborhood, we turned onto the gravel road that led toward the Scorpions' shack. All of a sudden I didn't feel so optimistic about the whole thing. The sun was still shining high in the sky, so there was plenty of daylight left. But I could feel my heart beating hard and my breathing got fast.

"What if they beat us to the shack?" I asked. "What if they're waiting for us?"

Wash stopped and gave me one of his classic disgusted looks. "How can they be waiting for us? We just saw them in the park."

"Maybe they took another road."

"Yeah," said Tony. "We don't know this side of the river. Maybe there's a back way or something."

"Look," said Wash, "even if they followed us, they'd have to cross the bridge—unless they wanted to swim, in which case the pollution in the river would probably kill them. And then they'd have to run full speed over some imaginary back way that probably doesn't even exist. So my personal opinion is that we're completely safe, but we better keep moving or else they really will catch us."

Wash turned away from us and half ran, half walked up the gravel road. Tony and I practically had to run full speed to keep up with him. It was twice as hard for us because we were carrying bats. In a few minutes we reached the place where the dirt road broke off up the hill to the Scorpions' shack. Wash was ready to run right up the hill, but I grabbed him from behind. "Wait a minute. Let's look around a little."

"For what?"

"I don't know. Signs—a light in the shack, footprints

113

on the road, whatever. We're detectives, Wash. We don't just rush in like a bunch of maniacs."

Wash nodded. I knew the part about being detectives would get him interested. "Okay, you're right, B.J. But let's be quick and efficient. You've got the best eyes for distance, so you check out the shack. Tony and I will look for footprints."

I scrunched down behind a bush and squinted up at the shack. The sun was in my eyes, so I pulled my cap down lower until I was just gazing under the bill. That helped a little, but it sure would have been nice to have Dr. Washington's binoculars. To be honest, I couldn't see much of anything. But at least I could tell that no one was moving around the shack, and it didn't look like anything was going on inside either. That made me feel a little better.

"Okay, I guess it's safe. But let's check the back window before we go in. You guys find anything?"

"There's a lot of footprints," said Tony, "but I can't tell if they're going up or going down. The dirt's too hard."

"What about you, Wash?" He was off to the side, right where the dirt road broke off from the gravel road.

"Naw," he said, "just a couple of candy wrappers. Snickers and Three Musketeers. The Snickers was pretty recent. Wait a minute." Wash walked up the gravel road and bent over to pick up something small. He held it close to his eyes, as if he were reading the fine print on a bubble gum cartoon. "Incredible!"

"What is it?"

"It's my bat!"

"What are you talking about?" If the thing in Wash's

hand was his bat, then some mad scientist was shrinking baseball equipment.

"I'm telling you, man, it's my bat! Come here and look at it." He was practically jumping with excitement.

Tony and I walked over to Wash and stared at the thing in his hand. It was a dirty white piece of fabric—about the size of a quarter—with ragged threads at the edges. It didn't look like a bat at all.

"I don't get it," said Tony.

"What is it?" I asked.

Wash looked at us like we were complete morons. "Don't you see? It's the tape from my bat. I'm positive."

"C'mon," said Tony, "it doesn't even look like tape."

"It could be tape," I said. "But how do you know it's from your bat?"

"I know. I just know. I taped it myself, B.J. It was some stuff from my dad's office, and it was just like this. I'm positive."

He looked up at me like he was waiting for me to agree with him. Tony was right—the tiny piece of fabric in Wash's hand didn't look much like tape, but it was so dirty and worn out that it didn't look like much of anything. Anyway it didn't matter what it looked like now. What mattered was that Medgar Washington—my very best friend—was absolutely positive that it was the tape from his bat. That was good enough for me.

"Okay," I said, "it's the tape from your bat. What do we do about it?"

Wash looked up the gravel road. It rose gradually for a couple hundred yards, and then it disappeared on the other side of the hill. "We find my bat," he said.

"But where?"

"There, over the hill."

"What about the shack?" asked Tony.

"Forget the shack. The tape was in the middle of the gravel road. Someone was carrying my bat on this road."

"But the tape could have blown over here," I pointed out. "Or it could have fallen off the bat weeks ago."

"It didn't," said Wash. "The bat's on the other side of that hill. I can feel it."

"Feel it?" asked Tony. "What happened to Mr. Logic?"

Wash shrugged and smiled. "Sometimes great detectives have to work from instinct. Let's go." With the tiny piece of fabric in his hand, he walked up the gravel road toward the hill. Tony and I looked at each other and shook our heads. Then we followed him. What else could we do? It was his bat, his tape, and his instinct.

As we approached the top of the hill, my heart started beating hard again. Only this time it wasn't from fear; it was from excitement. It was crazy, but I really believed Wash. The bat—and the solution to the mystery—was waiting right on the other side.

At first we couldn't see much of anything. To the right there were empty fields, and more hills, and more fields leading out toward the lake. To the left it looked pretty much the same—just fields and hills and more fields. And then we saw it.

Actually we heard it before we saw it. Screams and yells and *Hey, battah battah battah!* Right below us, down in a field that was almost hidden by the hill, were a bunch of kids playing baseball. Little kids—six, seven, eight years old. They were wearing white T-shirts with something

116

written across the front. I couldn't read it from the top of the hill. But I could see that they didn't have much equipment—a few gloves, a couple of bats, one batting helmet, and a catcher's mask. And I recognized the umpire. He was bigger and older than the rest, and he was wearing the uniform of Halbertson's Flowers. It was Nong Den.

"I don't believe it," I muttered. "It's impossible."

"My bat!" Wash exclaimed.

"Believe it," said Tony.

We ran down the hill toward the field. The kids were so busy playing baseball that they didn't notice us until we were right on top of them. The pitcher went into his windup and the batter dropped into his stance and cocked his bat—an aluminum bat with a silver top, a black bottom, and ragged white tape around the handle.

"That's my bat!" yelled Wash.

Suddenly the game stopped. Nong looked over at us from behind the plate. For a second his face got all screwed up and tight, and he made a move as if he was going to run away. But I guess he realized that it didn't matter if he ran or didn't run. He was caught.

"Time!" The game stopped as Nong walked toward us and tried to smile. "How you like my team?"

I looked out at the little kids. There were almost enough for two teams, really, but the fielders and hitters all had the same name written across their T-shirts in black Magic Marker: *Little Americans*.

"They're great," I said, "but they're using our equipment."

"They're using my bat," said Wash.

"How could you do this?" asked Tony.

Nong looked down at the ground. Then he looked out at the field. The Little Americans were all waiting for him, just like a Little League team would wait for an umpire who called time. "Go ahead and play," he said. "I gotta talk to these guys."

"I want my bat," Wash demanded. "Now."

"Let them finish the game," I said.

"Yeah," Tony agreed, "what difference does it make?"

Wash looked over at the kid in the batter's box. He was about half Wash's size, and he choked up past the top of the tape. But he had a pretty good batting stance, with both eyes focused right on the pitcher. Wash shrugged and smiled a little. Then he turned back to Nong. "Why'd you do it, man?"

Nong stared at the ground again. "I don't know, Wash. It's hard to explain. I want them to be Americans." He looked up and his face was very serious. "Real Americans. Like people on other side of the river. Like you guys. And real Americans got to play baseball. It's what you call . . . national . . ."

"Pastime," I said.

Nong smiled. "Yeah, national pastime. Real American kids got to play real baseball. But these kids, they got no money for bats and gloves and baseballs. So I figure I sort of borrow some from Little League."

"You mean steal," said Wash.

"No man, I swear—I gonna give everything back after the season."

"Why'd you take my bat?"

" 'Cause you rich, man. I figure you just buy another one."

Wash's face got all scrunched up, like just thinking about the whole thing was painful. "But it was special to me, Nong. It was more than just a bat."

"I know, Wash. I'm real sorry. But I didn't know when I took it. Then when you stop hitting I was gonna bring it back, but everything get so crazy. I was scared, y'know?"

"But you kept taking things," said Tony.

I ran down the list: "Obermeyer's glove, the practice ball, the catcher's mask . . ."

Nong stared down at the ground again. "A few other things too—from other teams."

"And then you stole your own bat," said Wash, "because you thought it would put us off the trail. Pretty clever, Nong."

Nong smiled kind of sadly and shook his head. "No man, I didn't even know you on the trail. I took my bat 'cause it's small. These kids pretty small, y'know?"

He turned away from us and looked out at the field. The kid at the plate was using Nong's bat—actually the Granada Little League's bat. It was definitely small, but he still had to choke up on it. The pitcher had Obermeyer's glove, but he sure didn't have Obermeyer's fastball. He just kind of lobbed it up there, and the batter smashed a solid grounder to short. The ball cut through the weeds like a fast-moving snake. The shortstop didn't have a glove, but he got down on it just the way you're supposed to, scooped it up barehanded, and threw to first in time to get the runner by two steps.

"Awesome," said Wash. "That kid can play."

Nong clapped his hands and shouted out to the shortstop. "That-a-way, Mop! Just the way we practice." Mop nodded seriously, like he heard the compliment, but he didn't even crack a smile. He just turned around to the outfield and flashed two fingers to let them know there were two outs. Then he got back into position and waited for the next pitch. Seven years old and the kid was already acting like a major leaguer.

I could tell that Nong was really proud of the Little Americans. And he had a right to be. The field was just a bunch of overgrown weeds, and most of the kids didn't have the right equipment. Some of them didn't even have shoes. But they were playing real baseball, good baseball. And Nong was their teacher.

Finally, he turned around and faced us. "So what you gonna do?" he asked.

"You have to return all the equipment," I said.

"Everything," ordered Tony.

"Today," said Wash. "As soon as the little guys finish the game."

"Sure. But what you gonna do to me? You gonna beat me up or something?"

We all looked at each other in surprise. Personally, that was the last thing on my mind, and I doubt that Wash or Tony was thinking about it either. "Of course not," I said. "Nobody's gonna beat you up. You're our teammate, Nong."

"Yeah," said Wash, "and what you're doing here is a good thing, man. It really is."

"But stealing isn't right," Tony pointed out. "Or borrowing, or whatever—it's just not right."

"No," I agreed, "it's definitely wrong. That's for sure."

"So what you gonna do to me?" Nong repeated. His

voice was sad and scared, but he seemed willing to go along with whatever we decided. So what were we going to decide?

No one said anything for a while. I guess we were all just thinking. Then Wash took off his glasses and polished them on his uniform shirt. "Look," he said, "this is not just our problem. It's a Granada Little League problem."

I stared at him in amazement. He sounded just like Mr. Farnsworth. "That's right. So what do we do?"

Wash fitted his glasses carefully around his ears and adjusted the nose bridge. Mr. Logic was back. "If it's a Granada Little League problem," he reasoned, "it should be settled by the commissioner. Let's talk to Dave."

13

We had been to Dave's house only once—the night we followed Crazy Pete—but we found it on the first try.

When we got to the porch, Wash jumped up the steps and rang the bell. Then he opened the screen door and gave a couple of loud raps on the heavy wooden door. On the second rap, the door opened, and Wash was face-to-face with Dave's hairy chest.

"Can I help you boys?" Dave was wearing dress shoes and a nice pair of slacks, but he was naked from the waist up. There was a big glob of shaving cream behind his left ear.

"Oh . . . uh . . . hi, Dave," said Wash. "I guess we caught you at a bad time."

Dave gave us the once over. We probably looked like a sidewalk sporting goods store. We each had a bat and our own glove, and everyone except Nong had cleats. Then there was the catcher's mask and the batting helmet and three practice balls and Obermeyer's glove and four other gloves. It didn't take Dave too long to figure out what was going on. "Come in," he said. "I've got a few minutes."

He led us through the entrance hall to a room in the back of the house. It was a study, I guess, with a desk and lots of shelves. There weren't enough chairs, so we just laid the equipment on the floor and stood in front of the desk. "I'll be back in a minute," said Dave. "I have to make a phone call."

While Dave was out of the room, we all looked around. Most of the shelves were filled with books, but there were a bunch of trophies too and a wooden plaque for being commissioner. One of the trophies caught my eye. It was a tall red column with a baseball player—a kid—on top. His bat was swung around in front, and his eyes were looking out as if he'd just popped one over the center-field fence. The inscription read: "David Harrelson, Most Valuable Player 1967, Granada Little League."

I didn't have a chance to show the other guys, because Dave came back in the room. He cleared some papers away from the front of his desk and sat on the edge. He was wearing an old T-shirt, and I noticed that the shaving cream was gone from his ear. "All right, gentlemen, what's this all about?"

"Gee, Dave," said Wash, "we're really sorry about bothering you. I guess you were going on a date or something."

Dave smiled. "Or something. Now, where'd you find the equipment?"

Dave listened carefully as Wash told him the whole story—the early investigations, the Black Scorpions, the tape in the road, and Nong and the Little Americans. Tony and I threw in a few comments too. Nong just stood and stared at the floor.

When we were finished, Dave sat and looked at us for a while. At first his eyes focused on Wash. Then on me and Tony. And then on Nong—for a long, long time. He didn't say anything, but I could tell he wasn't very happy about the situation. Finally, he started speaking in a quiet, sad voice.

"Boys, I've been associated with the Granada Little League for a long time, and I've always thought it was a very special program and a special experience for young people. I still believe that, but right now I don't feel much like being associated with the program—or any program—because I don't want to be in this position and I don't want to make this decision."

"But you're the commissioner," said Wash.

Dave shifted on the edge of the desk. "Yes, Wash, I am the commissioner. So I have to put my personal feelings aside. I have to forget how wrong it is for those little children to be so poor when the rest of this town is so rich. And I have to make the decision that is best for the Granada Little League. Mr. Den, step forward, please."

Nong stepped up and stood right in front of the desk. Nong is pretty short and Dave is pretty tall, so even though Dave was sitting down it seemed like he was towering over Nong.

"Tell me, Mr. Den, did you take this equipment?" Dave pointed to the bats, gloves, balls, batting helmet, and catcher's mask, all lying in a pile on the floor.

Nong didn't look at the equipment, and he didn't look

at Dave. He just stared at the bottom of the desk. "Yes, I took it."

"All of it?"

"All of it."

"Why?"

Nong looked up and gazed directly into Dave's eyes. "I try to help my people, Dave. The big kids—like the Scorpions—they angry all the time. Always talk about fighting and war in our country. But the little kids don't remember fighting. I think maybe they should just play baseball and be like Americans. It's the national pastime, y'know?"

Dave smiled, but it was the saddest smile I had ever seen. Maybe it was the late-afternoon sun coming through the window of the study, but it almost looked like he was crying. "Yes, Nong, I know."

He drummed his fingers on the desk, and I could tell that he was deciding the case in his mind. Finally he said, "Mr. Den, you are a truly remarkable young man. These boys could learn a lot from you about helping other people. But you can't help the poor by stealing from the rich. We have a story about that called Robin Hood, but that's all it is—a story. The fact is that we live in a nation of laws, and stealing is stealing no matter why you steal or who you steal from. Can you understand that?"

Nong looked back at the bottom of the desk. "Yeah, I understand," he said quietly. "Stealing is wrong. I guess I pretend it was just borrowing. But I don't fool anyone— even me."

Dave looked out the window at the sun. It was pretty

low in the sky, and we were all going to be late for dinner, including Dave and his date or something. But right then dinner didn't seem very important. Dave looked back at Nong and spoke in a soft but strong voice.

"Mr. Den, this is the most difficult decision I have ever made as commissioner of the Granada Little League. But I have no choice. You are suspended for the rest of the season, including the championship game."

"Dave!" cried Wash. "You can't do that!"

"Quiet, Mr. Washington. This is not your concern."

"But we need Nong against the Lions. He's our lead-off man!"

"I said quiet, Wash. Nong, do you have anything to say?"

Nong looked pretty scared. "You gonna put me in jail?" he asked.

Dave shook his head. "That's not my decision, Nong, but I don't think anyone's going to put you in jail. I will have to discuss this with the police, though, and they might want to ask you some questions. If they do, I'll be there to help you. I will also have to tell your parents."

"Sure. They gonna be pretty mad."

Dave smiled. "We'll talk to them together, okay?"

"Okay. Thanks, Dave. And, uh—I'm really sorry, y'know?"

"I know, Nong. So am I."

Dave slipped off the desk and stood above us. "Okay, gentlemen. I guess that's it. You can just leave the equipment where it is. Now if you'll excuse me, I have to finish getting dressed."

He walked toward the door. Tony, Nong, and I picked

up our personal equipment and followed him. Dave was about to turn off the light when he noticed Wash standing near the trophy shelf. His bat and glove and cleats were at his feet, and he was just kind of staring into space.

"Are you coming, Mr. Washington?"

At the sound of Dave's voice, Wash came back to earth. A giant grin spread across his face. "I've got a great idea!"

Dave kept his hand on the light switch. "Let's talk about it later, Wash. I really have to go."

"Please, Dave? It'll just take a minute—and it'll solve everything!"

Dave shook his head like he was sort of half disgusted and half amazed. Then he dropped his hand from the light switch and led us back across the room. "Okay, I'll give you a minute. But this better be good."

Wash took off his glasses and polished them on his uniform shirt. Then he hooked them back over his ears and adjusted the nose bridge. He had already used about thirty seconds, but he acted like he had all the time in the world. "Well," he began, "the way I look at it—Nong was trying to do the right thing, but he did it the wrong way."

Dave nodded. "A very astute assessment. Now what's your idea?"

"Well, maybe we can help him do it the right way."

Dave shifted on the edge of the desk and listened more intently. "Go on."

"What if we put together an equipment drive—you know, like a canned food drive or Toys for Tots, only instead of food or toys we would collect baseball equipment? I know lots of kids who have extra bats and gloves and stuff just lying around."

"That's a great idea!" I said. "I've got a glove that's just getting dusty in the garage. And I've got an old pair of baseball shoes too."

"My little brothers use my old bats and gloves," said Tony, "but we could give them a couple of practice balls—and I've got a ton of baseball hats up in my closet."

"You guys really do this?" asked Nong. "You really help my people?" He was smiling for the first time since we caught him with the stolen equipment.

"Sure," said Wash. "It'll be great. We'll have those Little Americans looking like real ball players. I'm telling you, Dave, it would really work. I know it would work."

Dave was smiling too. "It's a wonderful idea, Wash. And I'll do everything I can to help you make it work. I'll call a managers' meeting, and we'll set up some kind of system. Maybe we could have drop-off boxes at the games . . ."

"Or we could go to the kids' houses," said Wash.

"Or call them on the phone," I suggested.

"Or talk to them at the games," said Tony.

Dave put his hands up in the air. "Hold on—whoa! We have to sit down and organize this. Let me call some of the managers and talk to the board of directors, and I'll get back to you in a couple of days. Fair enough?"

"Yeah, sure, Dave. In the meantime we can do some planning too." Wash's brain was still clicking away.

"Fine. But don't do anything until you discuss it with me. Let's do the right thing the right way. Okay?"

"Okay."

"Promise?"

Wash nodded seriously. "I promise."

"We all promise," I said.

"Great." Dave hopped off the desk and headed for the door, but Wash stopped him in his tracks.

"Uh, Dave?"

"Yes, Wash?"

"What about Nong?"

"What about him?"

"Well, it seems to me that if Nong helps us with the equipment drive, he's doing community service work. And in the American legal system, community service work is sometimes used instead of other kinds of punishment. So maybe you could suspend Nong's sentence and let him play for the rest of the season."

Dave smiled and shook his head kind of sadly. "Mr. Washington, you are a very smart young man, and you'll probably make a good lawyer some day. But this is not a court of law. It's Little League. Playing Little League is a privilege. And when Nong broke the law he lost that privilege. I'm really sorry."

"But you said yourself he did it for the right reason. He was just trying to help his people."

"Forget it, Wash," said Nong. "I broke the law. I got to be punished."

"No, I won't forget it, Nong. It's not right. Look, Dave, America is the land of opportunity, right?"

Dave smiled. "Yes, Wash, that's right. At least that's the way it should be."

"And opportunity means having a chance to do something, right?" Wash was really going now.

"Right."

"And if you don't succeed at first, you should try, try again. Isn't that true?"

Dave was still smiling. "Yes, Wash, that's true."

"Well, then America is really the land of second chances. I mean what kind of opportunity is it if you can't try again? So what do you say, Dave? Give him a break. Please."

Dave shook his head—only it wasn't a "no" kind of head shake; it was more a "wow" kind of head shake, like he was amazed by the way Wash's mind worked. I was kind of amazed myself. I always knew that Wash was really smart, but this was the first time I'd ever seen him use his smartness for someone besides himself.

"I take back what I said about you being a good lawyer, Wash. You could be a *great* lawyer—or a judge—or whatever you want to be." Dave turned away from Wash and looked at Tony and me. "How do you two feel about this? Do you think I should give Nong a second chance?"

Tony and I looked at each other, but we didn't have to discuss it. "Yes," I said. "What Nong did was wrong, but he didn't mean to hurt anyone. He did it to help."

"Definitely," said Tony. "Let him play, Dave."

Dave sat down on the edge of the desk, drumming his fingers on the wood, looking at all four of us, one by one. It was hard to tell from his face what he was going to decide. Finally, he said, "Gentlemen, I probably shouldn't do this, but I'm going to let Nong play for the rest of the season—provided you all work together on the equipment drive."

"All right!"

"Thanks, Dave."

"Yeah, thanks a lot."

"You won't be sorry."

"I hope not. Now let's get out of here."

Dave led us through the hallway to the front door. He stood on the porch for a few seconds, watching us walk down the path. Then he went inside to get ready for his date or something.

Out on the sidewalk, Nong flashed us a big smile. "Thanks guys, for sticking up for me and everything."

"That's okay," I said. "You're our teammate—we've all gotta stick together."

"Yeah," Tony added. "You and Emily are the only ones who've been hitting lately. Maybe now we can all hit together."

"Listen, Nong," said Wash, "we've got this kind of club, you know. It's called the Sluggers Club. So far it's just Tony, B.J., and me. But since we're all going to be working together on the equipment drive, I was wondering if maybe you'd like to be a member of the club too. Of course, the other guys have to approve and everything."

"Fine with me," I said. "I think it's great."

"Yeah," Tony agreed, "definitely."

"I would be honored to join," said Nong, "but I'm not a slugger."

Wash grinned and put his arm around Nong's shoulders. "You are now," he said.

14

The equipment drive was a humongous success. In two weeks, we collected enough bats, balls, gloves, shoes, and baseball caps to supply two teams. The Granada Little League donated catcher's equipment, umpire's equipment, bases, and six batting helmets. Everyone was really generous. It made me proud to live in Granada.

I have to give the Sluggers Club a little credit too. Actually a lot of credit—I'm trying to be modest. The truth is that we worked harder than any of us had ever worked before. Instead of just picking one way to collect equipment, we used everybody's ideas and covered all the bases.

We had a big drop box behind the backstop—just like Dave suggested. Nong made a giant sign explaining about the Little Americans, and he even had a Polaroid picture of the team. The Sluggers Club went to every game and talked to the kids about donating their equipment—that was Tony's idea. Then we called them on the phone to remind them—that was my idea. Finally, we went to their houses and picked up their donations in person—that was Wash's plan.

We were always very polite, but we were aggressive too. Like I said, people were mostly generous, but a few kids acted like they were too busy to look for something to donate. We kind of insisted that they take the time. It's amazing what people have lying around in their closets and garages.

When we weren't collecting equipment, we were winning baseball games. As soon as Wash stepped up to the plate with his special bat, it was just like old times. The Sluggers Club went on a rampage, pounding balls all over the field and out of the field too. We won our last three games of the season, including the suspended game with Frangionni's Pizza, and finished the second half at 3 and 5. It was a pretty miserable record, but we were on a roll going into the championship game.

After the last game of the regular season, we loaded all the equipment into Dave's station wagon and headed across the river. It was a short drive, really—it only took us about ten minutes from our ballpark to the overgrown field where the Little Americans played. Along the way we passed the same big family sitting on their porch. I waved out the window and they waved back.

Dave looked at me in the rearview mirror. "Do you know those people, B.J.?"

"Yeah—sort of. I guess you could say we're acquaintances."

We passed the Black Scorpions' shack and drove up the gravel road. When we were on the other side, Dave turned down a dirt road that took us right to the field. Nong was already there with the Little Americans. They were all lined up in a neat row, with Nong standing in front. Danny was there too. I guess Nong needed an assistant coach now, because it definitely looked like he'd picked up a few new players.

Dave stopped the car and we all piled out. "Hey Nong!" shouted Wash. "How many teams you got here?"

Nong smiled and shrugged. "Just one team," he said, "but we got A and B squads."

"Yeah, and maybe C and D squads too."

We had five boxes of equipment in the back of Dave's car. Two of them were filled with general stuff for the team: bats, helmets, balls, bases, and the catcher's equipment. Dave and Nong took those boxes, and Dave helped him unpack, showing him what was what—kind of like one commissioner to another.

The other three boxes were full of stuff that we were giving to the players. Wash, Tony, and I lifted them from the back of the car and carried them over to one end of the line. The Little Americans jumped up and down trying to see what was in the boxes, but Danny got them settled down, and to tell you the truth, they waited pretty patiently for a bunch of little kids. Nong definitely had them trained.

We started with Pouk, a real little guy about six years old. Tony reached into the first box and pulled out an official Granada Little League cap with a big G on the front. We get a new one every year, so it was easy to collect lots of them. Tony set the cap on Pouk's head, but it was way too big—you couldn't even see his eyes. So Tony reached back into the box and found a smaller one. It was still too big, but it was the best we could do. And the little guy didn't seem to mind at all.

Next I reached into the second box and found a pair of tennis shoes. They were actually in pretty good shape— probably some kid had outgrown them and his parents stuck them in a closet. Pouk sat down on the ground and tried them on. They were big, but they were better than what he was wearing, which was nothing. It's tough to play baseball barefoot.

Finally, Wash reached into the third box and pulled out a glove. It was a small black one with white stitching. Pouk tried it on, and well—you know what they say—it fit like a glove. Wash has a good eye for equipment. I guess he saw it in the box and figured it was just right for this particular kid. Which it was.

Pouk pounded the palm a couple of times and broke into a big beautiful grin. "Thanks a lot," he said. "Now I gonna make all the plays!" That grin was really something. I think I'd give up a long home run just to frame it and put it on my wall.

We went down the line, dragging our three boxes along, and giving each of the Little Americans a cap, a pair of shoes, and a glove. Actually some of the kids were already wearing pretty good shoes, so we skipped over them and gave our best shoes to the kids who really needed them. No one was jealous or anything. Everyone got in the spirit of being generous and helping each other out. It was just like Christmas.

As we got down toward the end of the line, though, I started getting nervous. Like I said, we had plenty of caps, and we had enough shoes for the kids who really needed them. But we wanted to give every Little American a glove. That was the most important of all the gifts, because you can't play hardball without a glove. And Wash's box was looking pretty empty.

Sure enough, we ran out of gloves with one more kid to go. It was Mop, the great little shortstop. And the look on his face almost washed out Pouk's smile.

"I'm sorry," I said, "we didn't know there would be so many new players."

Mop tried to look tough. "That's okay. I don't need a glove."

"It's not right," said Wash. He stared back down into the box, as if there was one last glove hiding in the bottom.

"What's the matter?" asked Dave. He and Nong left the other equipment and came over to join us.

"We ran out of gloves," said Tony.

"That's too bad. Maybe we can find another one."

"I'm really sorry, Mop," said Nong. "Too many kids show up. But I can't say no. I can't tell them go away."

Mop looked down at the ground. "That's okay. I not angry at you, Nong. You the coach."

"Wait a minute," said Wash. "Wait just a minute." He ran back over to the car, opened the front door, and reached down for something on the floor. When he came out, he was holding his glove in his hand. He ran back and handed the glove to Mop. "Here," he said, "from one shortstop to another."

Mop took the glove and gazed at it as if it were a precious jewel. It was a beautiful glove, all soft brown leather, oiled and broken in by Wash. The palm looked like it was just waiting to scoop up every ground ball in sight. It probably cost about eighty dollars in a store, but the way Wash works in a glove it was worth even more.

"Thank you," said Mop, "but this too much."

"You can't do that, Wash," said Dave. "It's practically a brand-new glove, and I know how expensive it is."

Wash shrugged. "I already did it."

"We can find another one for him—another used one."

"Look, Dave," said Wash, "this little guy is the best shortstop I've ever seen. He's even better than I was at his age. He deserves a glove like that. Anyway, I've got another one almost like it at home."

"What about the championship game?" asked Tony. "I mean it's really generous, but we still gotta play the Lions."

Wash shook his head. "It's not like my bat. I can field with my other glove just as well as I field with this one. The Lions won't get anything past me—I promise." He turned and smiled at Mop. "You're welcome—now show me how you scoop."

Mop broke into a huge grin and ran out toward shortstop. The rest of the Little Americans followed him. Nong must have already had them organized into two teams, because about half went out in the field and the other half stayed in to bat. A few of the littlest guys just hung around by the sidelines. I guess they were riding the aluminum—only it was more like riding the weeds.

We all helped Nong get the bases into place. In the meantime, the catcher put on his equipment and the first batters picked up their bats and helmets. When everything was set, Nong slipped on his chest protector and mask, took his place behind the catcher, and called out, "Play ball!"

Dave stood with us and watched the Little Americans do their stuff, and he was just as impressed as we were. There were a lot of good players out there. Mop was definitely the best fielder, though. In the second inning, he went for a ball in the hole, stabbed it backhanded, and made the long, hard throw across the diamond. The first baseman stretched and caught it just before the runner touched the bag.

"See what I mean!" Wash exclaimed. "Mop could play in Little League right now. He's better than half the shortstops."

"Hey," said Tony, "the first baseman made a pretty good stretch. You gotta give him some credit too."

"I give everyone credit," said Dave. "You boys, the Little Americans, Nong . . ."

"Especially Nong," said Wash. "He teaches them real baseball—the right way."

"Absolutely," Dave agreed. "These players will be a real asset to the Granada Little League."

"Look who's here." Out of the corner of my eye, I'd noticed a flash of movement on top of the hill. When I turned to see what it was, my heart started beating hard in my chest. It was the Black Scorpions, lined up along the crest of the hill like some weird army. They were carrying all kinds of rusty weapons—at least they looked like weapons to me: a long-handled ax, a couple of sharp-toothed rakes, a hoe, and a couple of heavy metal shovels. And right in the middle was Mr. Big Knife, carrying a huge, wicked-looking scythe—just like the Grim Reaper holds in pictures. I don't know much about the Grim Reaper, but

I knew enough about Mr. Big Knife to get very nervous. That giant scythe made his knife look like a toy.

"Trouble," whispered Tony.

"They're gonna spoil everything," I muttered.

"I knew they were bad news," said Wash.

"Wait," said Dave, "let's hear what they have to say."

It didn't look to me like they were going to say anything. It looked like they were just going to walk down the hill and kill us. If Dave hadn't been there, I would have started running and never stopped until I dropped dead from exhaustion—dropping dead was better than having my head chopped off by that scythe. But for some reason, Dave made me feel safe—sort of.

The Scorpions walked down the dirt road toward the field. When they were about halfway down, Nong noticed that we were staring at something. Then he noticed what we were staring at. He called time and walked over to join us. The Little Americans froze in their places. Nobody moved at all.

Mr. Big Knife approached us at the head of the little army. That scythe looked even sharper and bigger up close than it did at a distance. "Hey Little League boys!" he shouted. "Mr. Umpire! This very big day on our side of river."

"What can we do for you?" Dave's voice was calm and even.

"Do for me, Mr. Umpire? You can't do nothing for me. We gonna do something for you." Mr. Big Knife looked past us toward the Little Americans standing like a frozen baseball game out in the overgrown field. I could see his

139

eyes take in the whole picture at once. Then he looked from kid to kid as if he were examining them—or trying to intimidate them. In the whole field there wasn't a single sound, except maybe the pounding of my heart.

Still looking out at the field, Mr. Big Knife's cruel, handsome face contorted into that cold, deadly grin. "Looking good," he said, "looking very good." I couldn't tell if he was being sarcastic or serious. Then all of a sudden his grin got bigger and broader, and it didn't look cold or deadly at all. It just looked like a nice big smile. "But a good-looking team got to have a good-looking field. We gonna clean this place up. When we done, this field gonna look like official Little League park."

Mr. Big Knife walked right past us toward the edge of the field. He said something to a couple of the Little Americans and waited until the little guys got out of the way. When it was all clear, he brought that huge scythe back over his shoulder, hesitated for a split second, and then— whack!—he started chopping down the weeds.

15

The championship game was a week later, on Saturday afternoon. It was a beautiful day—bright and sunny but not too hot. Perfect for a ball game. And the park was really spruced up. The backstop was decorated with red, white, and blue banners, sort of like a giant American flag. There was a special desk for the official scorer and the announcer, and an extra set of stands on each side. The stands were packed ten minutes before game time; it seemed like everybody in Granada was there.

The Little Americans sat in the top row of our stands, wearing their official Granada Little League hats and their Little Americans T-shirts. They all had their gloves—just like kids who go to a big-league game and hope to catch a foul ball. Crazy Pete was there too. He looked sober and smelled clean—like he had taken a shower for the occasion.

We were all nervous before the game, but we were confident too. During the regular season, we had beaten the

Lions with Wash's bat, and we only lost to them after the bat disappeared. Now that the bat was back, we figured we had a good chance to put them away. Wash made us feel even more confident when he called us all together right before the game. We'd forgotten about our pregame ritual during the last half of the season. But now was the time to bring it back.

The whole team stood in a circle along the third-base line. Wash put his right hand into the center and clenched his fist hard and strong. Then I put my hand on top of Wash's, and Tony put his hand on top of mine. Then came Nong and Emily and all the other players until we were just one big stack of hands. Wash looked around the circle, focusing on each of us one by one. He didn't say anything, but we all knew what he meant. Finally he asked, "Who's gonna do it?" And we all shouted, "Flowers!"

We were the home team, so we trotted out to our positions. Naturally Wash was at shortstop and Tony at first base. Nong was in center field and Emily at second. But the big surprise was me: I was the man on the mound.

Like I said, I'm not a bad pitcher or anything. In fact, I was 5 and 2 on the season. But I got totally clobbered the last time we played the Lions; I didn't even get an out. I guess Mr. Farnsworth figured he'd start with me and bring in Roger Pettinger if I got in trouble. Anyway, it was B.J. Grady against our old buddy Edward Obermeyer.

Dave the ump handed the game ball to our catcher, who tossed it out to me. I took a few last warm-up tosses and nodded that I was ready. Actually I wasn't ready at all. My heart was beating hard, and I felt like I could barely breathe. But it was just nerves. I figured I'd calm down once the game started.

"Play ball!" Dave shouted.

"Now batting for the Lions Club: Rory Mendoza." The announcer's voice boomed across the field. It was really weird having an announcer—sort of like being in the big leagues. To tell you the truth, it made me even more nervous.

I leaned forward for the sign. Actually I didn't need a sign, because I only have two pitches: a fastball and a change-up. It's pretty ridiculous to throw a change-up on the first pitch of the game because there's nothing to change from. So it was fastball all the way. I wound up and let go of a good hard one. In fact, I was so pumped up that it was one of the fastest fastballs I ever threw. The only problem was that it hit Rory Mendoza right in the shoulder. Ouch!

I stepped toward the plate and stared at Mendoza lying on the ground. He was rubbing his shoulder, but it didn't look too bad. "Are you okay?" I asked.

He nodded and got to his feet with a hand from the number-two hitter. Then he trotted on down to first.

I walked back to the mound and tried to calm down, but I just got more nervous. Now I was practically gulping for air. It always bothers me when I hit a batter, but it was ten times worse to do it on the very first pitch of the championship game of my last season of Little League in front of the whole town.

"Let's go, B.J.!" shouted Mr. Farnsworth.

"C'mon, B.J.," called Wash, "get tough."

"Yay B.J.! Yay B.J.!" My mom is always an optimist.

"Now batting for the Lions Club: Jimmy Samuels."

I was so frustrated that I didn't even bother leaning forward for the sign. I just went right into my windup, but I started so fast that I got kind of confused—I just didn't have any rhythm. So I stopped in the middle and tried to get myself straightened out.

"Balk!" Dave the ump motioned Mendoza down to second. I didn't bother to argue. I knew he was right. A pitcher can't stop in the middle of his motion, but I was so screwed up that I didn't have any choice.

All of a sudden I was surrounded on the mound. Wash, Tony, and Emily were all staring at me like I had the bubonic plague. "What's the matter, B.J.?" asked Tony. "Do you feel okay?"

"Yeah," I mumbled, "I'm okay. A little nervous, I guess." That was one of the greatest understatements of my life.

Wash grabbed my arm. "Look at me, B.J.," he demanded. The sun was shining off his goggles, but I could still see his eyes, calm and strong and intelligent. "You're a good pitcher, B.J. You're a slugger *and* a pitcher. Maybe I never told you that before, but I'm telling you now. I have complete confidence in you. Do you hear me?"

"Yeah, I hear you."

"Do you believe me?"

"Yeah."

"Good, now kick some butt." Wash and Tony ran back to their positions. I was alone with Emily—alone except that everyone was watching.

"Listen, B.J., I want to win this game just as much as

you do. But no matter what happens, I want you to know that I think you're really special. The way you guys helped those kids makes me proud just to be your teammate." She looked up at me with a really nice smile, and for a weird moment I thought she was going to kiss me, right there on the pitcher's mound in front of the whole town.

"Let's go," yelled Dave the ump. "Play ball!"

Emily trotted back to second base. I stepped on the rubber, squeezed the ball in my right hand, and leaned forward for the sign. I was still nervous, but I felt better—a lot better. I wound up and fired a fastball right down the middle.

"Steee-rike one!"

I fired another fastball that just missed on the outside. Then I tried a change-up that made the poor guy look silly.

"Steee-rike two!"

I was ahead in the count 1 and 2, so I decided to make him swing at an outside fastball. He barely got a piece of it and hit a dribbler toward the right side. Emily threw him out with plenty of time to spare, but the man on second went to third. There was one out.

Now I was facing the meat of the Lions order. The last time I saw them, they hammered me so hard that Mr. Farnsworth had to bring in artificial resuscitation. But last time was last time, and this time was this time. On a 1-and-1 fastball, their number-three man lifted a high pop fly to center field. Nong got under it and waited. Rory Mendoza waited at third base with one foot on the bag. I waited too—ready to duck or take the relay. Finally the ball plopped into Nong's glove and Rory took off at full speed. Nong made a great one-hop throw to our catcher, and Rory Mendoza slid in a cloud of dust. It looked close to me, but Dave the ump was right on top of it.

"Safe!" We were down 1–0.

I got the cleanup hitter on a grounder to short. It was kind of a tough play, but Wash made it look easy. As we ran back to the dugout, he patted me on the back. "Great job, B.J. Don't worry about the run. We'll get lots of 'em."

"I'm not worried." I wasn't either. Not the way the Sluggers Club had been hitting since we found Wash's bat. One run was nothing. I figured we'd get it back in the first inning. The only thing is, I didn't figure on Obermeyer. He was throwing smoke, and he was right on the money. He mowed Nong down with three pitches and got Emily with three more. Wash took him to a full count, but then Obermeyer let loose a fastball that made my stuff look slow. Wash swung late and tapped a grounder to the first baseman. Three up, three down.

I trotted back out to the mound and took a few warm-up tosses. After watching Obermeyer, I knew I had to get tough. And that's exactly what I did. For the next five innings, I pitched the game of my life. My fastball was hopping, and it was right around the plate. Control is the secret for a Little League pitcher—for any pitcher—and if you've got control and velocity, you're cruising.

Unfortunately, old Edward Obermeyer was cruising too. I have to give the guy credit—he's a jerk and a moron, but he's got a great arm. When he's hot, he's very hot.

The score was still 1–0 going into the bottom of the sixth. It was a heck of a game, a real pitchers' duel. The only difference between the Flowers and the Lions was my nervous freak-out in the first inning. But I couldn't think about that now. We had one more shot. The game—the championship—the whole season—was on the line.

Our number-nine hitter led off the inning. It was the kind of situation where a big-league manager would send up a pinch hitter, but Mr. Farnsworth didn't have anyone better, so he let the poor guy hit. Obermeyer blew him away with three pitches.

"Now batting for the Flowers: Nong Den!"

"C'mon, Nong!" I yelled. "Get something going."

"Make him pitch to you, Nong!" yelled Mr. Farnsworth. He ran his hand through his hair and across his face. Then he tweaked his nose, pulled his right ear, shook his head, and brushed his jacket. Most of it was just nervousness, but the nose was the take sign.

Nong stepped into the box and made his strike zone as small as possible. Obermeyer went into his windup, and the Lions infield started chattering: *Hey, battah battah! Hey, battah battah!* Nong watched a hard fastball just miss the outside corner.

"That-a-way, Nong!" shouted Mr. Farnsworth. "Wait for your pitch!" He did a bunch of weird nervous things, and Nong tried to figure out the sign. Actually everyone in the park knew he was taking—at least anyone who knew about baseball. With Nong's speed on the base paths, a walk was practically a double.

Hey, battah battah! Hey, battah battah! Obermeyer fired another fastball that cut the plate in half—right at Nong's eyes. Ball two.

"Make him pitch to you, Nong!"

"We have visitors," said Tony. I looked toward the first-base side. The Black Scorpions were walking in front of the stands toward their favorite spot behind the backstop.

"I wonder why they're so late. I mean they came to every other game."

"Maybe it's no fun anymore," Wash suggested. "Y'know, now that they decided to be good guys."

"Steee-rike one!" Nong watched a fastball right down the middle.

"Steee-rike two!" Nong watched another one. Then Obermeyer missed outside. It was a full count, and Nong had never lifted the bat from his shoulder.

Obermeyer leaned in for the sign and went into his windup. The Lions infield chattered behind him: *Hey, battah battah! Hey, battah battah!* Then just as Obermeyer was about to deliver the pitch, the Black Scorpions started chanting in loud obnoxious voices that cut through the chatter of the infield: "Obie! Obie! Obie! Obie!" I don't know if Obermeyer noticed them, but the pitch was a foot high. We had a man on first.

"What do you know?" asked Wash. "They're on our side."

"Now batting for the Flowers: Emily Kravitz!"

"C'mon, Emily! Move him along!" Emily looked down at Mr. Farnsworth and tried to decipher the sign. It was a little confusing, because he threw in about twenty extra nervous movements, but it looked to me like she was taking all the way.

Sure enough, Emily watched the first pitch go by—right down the middle. As soon as it reached the plate Nong Den took off from first. The Lions catcher pegged it down, but it wasn't even close. Now we had a man in scoring position.

"All right, Nong!" I shouted. "Way to put the pressure on!"

The next pitch was another hard fastball right down the pike. Emily took a cut at it and missed by a foot.

"Steee-rike two!"

"She doesn't have the bat speed," said Tony. "He's gonna blow her away."

"He's blowing everyone away."

Emily tapped her bat three times on the outside of the plate. Then she lifted the bat above her head, wiggled her shoulders, and dropped down into her stance. She looked a little scared, but she looked tough too.

Out on the mound, Obermeyer checked Nong and went into his windup. *Hey, battah battah! Hey, battah battah!* The pitch was hard and a little high. Emily swung late, but she made solid contact and smashed a line drive down the third-base line. It looked like a sure double—and a tie game—but the third baseman took off like he had springs in his shoes, and the ball landed smack in the palm of his glove. Nong was already halfway to third, and suddenly Emily's sure double looked like a sure double play and the end of the game. But Nong slammed on the brakes and dove back to the bag just in time to beat the throw.

On the bench, I felt like I lived and died and came back to life in about two seconds. "Heart-attack city," I mumbled.

"She was robbed," said Tony.

Emily ran back into the dugout and threw down her batting helmet. Her face was red and disgusted. "Hey c'mon, Emily," I said, "you pounded it."

"You can't hit it any better than that," said Tony.

"It's not fair," Emily moaned, sitting down beside me. "You pitched a great game, B.J. It's just not fair."

"At least we're still alive."

"Now batting for the Flowers: Medgar Washington!"

"C'mon, Wash!" yelled Mr. Farnsworth. "Show us how!" He didn't bother to flash any signs—Wash understood the situation perfectly, and he knew exactly what to do. There were two outs, a fast man on second, and we were one run down in the bottom of the last inning of the championship game of the last year of our Little League careers. A single would tie the game. Just one solid single from the greatest hitter in the Granada Little League. That wasn't much to ask. Was it?

I got up from the dugout bench and walked over to the on-deck circle. If Wash singled, the rest would be up to me. "Do it, Wash!" I yelled. "Please," I whispered.

Wash stepped into the box and held his black-and-silver bat tightly in his hands. The white tape on the handle was still torn, just the way we found it. Wash said he didn't want to cover up any of the hits with new tape. I told him he was completely insane, but at that particular moment I was willing to believe anything—as long as he had one more hit in that bat.

Wash took a couple of practice swings and smiled out at the mound. "C'mon, Edward, lay it on me!"

Obermeyer just grunted and fingered the ball behind his back. I have no idea what goes on in the mind of a moron like Ed Obermeyer, but I suppose he was thinking of all the times that Wash had beaten him and that he wasn't going to beat him this time. Anyway, he checked Nong at second, stepped toward the plate, and went into his windup. The infield started their stupid chatter: *Hey, battah battah! Hey, battah battah battah!*

Obermeyer snapped his arm forward and fired a high hard inside fastball that tailed off toward Wash's head. Wash hit the dirt and the ball sailed into the backstop right in front of Mr. Big Knife's face. He jumped back and broke into that weird smile of his. I didn't think it was deadly anymore. It was more like sarcastic.

Wash picked himself up and brushed off the dust. He didn't look intimidated or anything—just dirty. He lifted his batting helmet and adjusted his goggles. Then he yelled out at the mound, "Trying to kill me, Edward? Afraid to pitch to me?"

Obermeyer scowled and hissed. "I'm not afraid of anyone, Washington."

"Let's play baseball," ordered Dave the ump. "We can have a discussion group later."

Wash was about to step back into the box when a loud obnoxious voice pierced through the noise of the crowd: "Little League boy! Little League boy!" It was Mr. Big Knife.

Wash turned toward the backstop. Now he looked sort of pissed off. It's funny—he didn't mind the fastball at his head because that was just baseball. But the Black Scorpions were something else.

"What do you want, man? I'm busy."

Mr. Big Knife's handsome face was framed by the red, white, and blue banners that decorated the backstop. "Take him deep, baby. You the man!"

It was the worst possible advice. All we needed was a single to stay in the game. A homer that comes up short is just a long out, and a long out would be the end of the season. But Wash broke into a big grin and said, "I'll show you deep."

He stepped back into the box, gripped the torn white tape on his bat, took a couple of level swings, and waited for the pitch. Obermeyer stepped toward the plate and went into his windup. The infield chattered like monkey maniacs: *Hey, battah battah! Hey, battah battah! Hey, battah battah battah!*

In the on-deck circle, I mumbled to myself, "Please, Wash. Please, just a single. Forget deep. Forget it." I looked up and realized Emily Kravitz was staring at me. She smiled and I smiled, and then we both looked back at the field.

Obermeyer snapped his arm forward and fired another high inside fastball. Only this one wasn't high enough, and it wasn't inside enough. It sailed toward the inner part of the plate right above Wash's waist—right in the zone. Wash's eyes lit up like a kid at Christmas. He stepped into the pitch, whipped his bat around, and caught it in the meat. Kablooom! The ball exploded like a shooting star over Obermeyer's head, over the center fielder's head, over the center-field fence, over the scoreboard, over the old tree, and out toward Falcon Street.

To tell you the truth I never saw it come down. Maybe that's because I was too busy yelling and screaming and watching Nong Den jump on the plate and Wash circle the bases and poor old Obermeyer throw his glove on the ground. Or maybe it's because Emily Kravitz ran into the on-deck circle and hugged me and kissed me right smack on the cheek. Or maybe it's because the Little Americans stormed our dugout like berserk big-league fans. Maybe it was all those reasons. Or maybe it was none of them. Maybe I never saw that ball come down because it didn't.

It's a crazy idea—I know it and I admit it—but sometimes I think that ball just kept sailing and sailing down Falcon Street, over Dave the ump's house, across the broken-down bridge, above the Cambodian neighborhood, past the Scorpions' shack, up the gravel road, and over the hill until it finally landed like a falling star in the brand-new baseball field on the other side of the river.